SUCCESS: STORIES

David A. Taylor

Washington Writers' Publishing House
Washington, DC

Copyright © 2008 by David A. Taylor

COVER DESIGN by Zamore Design
BOOK DESIGN by Barbara Shaw and David A. Taylor
TYPESETTING by Barbara Shaw
COVER PHOTOGRAPH by Frits Berends

LIBRARY OF CONGRESS CATALOGUING-IN-PUBLICATION DATA
Taylor, David A., 1961-
    Success : stories / David A. Taylor.
        p. cm.
    ISBN 978-0-931846-90-8
    1. Short stories, American. I. Title.
    PS3602.A94S83 2008
    813'.6—dc22

                                            2008015669

Printed in the United States of America

WASHINGTON WRITERS' PUBLISHING HOUSE
P. O. Box 15271
Washington, D.C. 20003

To Lisa

CONTENTS

ACKNOWLEDGEMENTS

I have received invaluable encouragement and counsel from many people, including: Richard Bausch, in his Heritage Writers Workshop at George Mason University and at the Bread Loaf Writers' Conference; Kate Blackwell and Richard Peabody, in workshops at the Writer's Center in Bethesda, Maryland; Peter Ho Davies and Alice Mattison at the Fine Arts Work Center in Provincetown; and my writing group in Washington, DC — Brendan Short, Buzz Mauro, and Robert Williams. Stories in this collection have appeared elsewhere, some in slightly different form: "Strikers" in *Baltimore Review*; "Strange Cabbages" in *Potpourri*; "Pelagro" and "Errand" in *Eclectica*; "May Day" in *Jabberwock Review*; "Child Thief" in *Potomac Review*; "Saigon Haircut" in *Fodderwing*; "Coral, from the Sea" in *Pindeldyboz*; "Counterfeit" in *Muse Apprentice Guild*; "Bottle" in *Zone 3*; "Electrolysis" in *Main Street Rag*; "Special Economic Zone: Shantou" in *Gargoyle*; "Success" in *Rio Grande Review*; and "Angelina Before the Throne of Heaven" in *The William & Mary Review*. I am grateful to everyone at Washington Writers' Publishing House, in particular Elisavietta Ritchie and Laura Brylawski-Miller.

Where is the warm summer's day when first
I saw the green-carpeted earth revolving and
men and women moving like panthers? . . .
The world has become a mystic maze erected
by a gang of carpenters during the night.

— Henry Miller

STRIKERS

HENDERSON is windmilling the green-and-red bowling ball over his head, his tongue poking out of his mouth.

"Watch me, boys!" he drawls.

He lets fly and halfway down the polished wood it kerflops into the gutter.

"Yeah, buddy," I say, "that's a clapper."

I'm already sick of all the jokes about our privates. But we can't help it. We're all too curious about which of us are the real Gonorrhea Strikers and which are merely the Placebo Breathers. Henderson picks up another ball and flings it down the lane, it clips a couple of pins.

"That a two, Henderson?" Puccini says.

Henderson slumps into the plastic chair, folds his arms across his chest. "How can I bowl with all this goddamn noise?"

"Fluoroquinolones!" I say.

Blank looks.

"You know what penicillin resistance means, don't you, boys?"

"Warner, shut up," says Puccini in the scorer's chair. "We're trying to relax here. Trying to win a game." He shoves his open hand toward the alley, like I have to be shown.

"It means they're shooting us up with the hard stuff," I say. "Resistant strain. Stuff that penicillin can't handle."

"Inski, you're up," Puccini says.

"And they're testing what?" I say. Nobody answers. "Grepafloxacin?"

Blank looks. The brutal, echoing crash of pins. Inski comes back hissing, "Yesss!"

THE ANNOUNCEMENT in *Guinea Pig Zero*, the must-read zine for clinical trial volunteers, had been more vague than usual. It called for males between 30 and 55 who could devote two weeks to help stamp out an un-named disease. The honorarium was higher than the norm ("up to $1,800 dollars!"), and the phone number seemed to be a line on the Hopkins campus. I was suspicious, and intrigued.

Dr. Gordon cleared things up the first day. "By helping this study," she said, "you'll help a lot of people who don't even know they have gonorrhea yet."

A third of us would get shot up with a penicillin-resistant strain, a third would get a strain resistant to tetracycline, and a third would get no virus at all—the pathetic "control group," for whom neither of the two new oral meds (grepafloxacin and cefixime) would have any benefit. In fact, they might make them sick. Precious.

Then they'd divide us again to see which of the drugs worked for which resistance. Randomization? Ask an experimental design wiz.

Dr. Gordon explained all this seated on her desk, blue suit, legs crossed. We were around her in a circle like a hive of worker bees. She had a forefinger raised, ticking off symptoms we could expect.

"First, you may feel pain during urination."

"What kind of pain?" I asked. "Stinging, dull, throbbing—"

"Stinging, mostly."

"How far up? All the way up my shank or—"

She laughed. "It depends, Allen. You'll know."

So she hated me. Fine. Someone's got to find out these things. The rest of those slugs were paralyzed. Perfect fodder for clinical trials. She ticked off another finger.

"Second, you may experience an oozy discharge from the urethra."

Old Mr. Lee leaned forward. "The what?"

"From your dick, pops," I said, loud enough for the old Chinaman to hear.

"Oh." He sat back, hands crossed.

"Will that hurt too?" Henderson said. So at least he was curious.

"No, hardly at all. And rest assured, as soon as you experience these symptoms and come to me, we'll give you stronger antibiotics to take care of it. We have no interest in watching you dangle."

She said. Smiling as if it was a crazy paranoid male fixation.

DR. GORDON showed us the gym. Smooth, like always: lay out the tough facts first, then show us the perks.

"Pain during urination," Henderson muttered. "Are all trials like this?"

I counted to ten, to let someone else go first. I get tired of always being the answer man. But no one said anything.

"No," I said. "I've been in fifteen studies, six of them here at Hopkins. Not one ever announced that kind of pain at the outset."

"I thought they'd licked gonorrhea years ago." Henderson sounded like he was from Glen Burnie or further south. Trying to cover it.

"You heard what she said," I said. "Gonorrhea's up thirty percent in the last nine years. We should buy stock."

The shiny wood flooring stretched across three basketball courts. A young woman in neon was running the circuit of the indoor track. In one corner, there was a creaky metal set of universal weights and some Nautilus stations. Henderson paused at the crunch machine, put his hand on its black seatcover.

"Pretty nice, eh?" he said, looking up at me. A kind of scared calmness in his eyes, a John Malkovich jaw.

"It's why I'm here." I smiled.

The guy with the crewcut walked up to Henderson.

"Name's Puccini. Bob Puccini. Yeah, y'know I was *hoping* we'd get to get in shape during this. I never have time otherwise."

"Right," I said, and turned to the personal notes on the bulletin board. "We all have busy schedules."

"This is my fourth study," Puccini said, ignoring me. "Every time I feel this buzz, like I'm Jonas Salk."

I snorted. We followed Dr. Gordon down the hall toward a sign for 'swimming pool.'

"Ah, I forgot," she said, turning on a three-inch heel. "Gentlemen, I'm afraid because of the nature of this study, we can't let you use the swimming pool."

"Why's that, doc?" Henderson said.

For the first time Dr. Gordon looked ruffled. "It's the sensitivity of the disease, not that there's any risk—"

"Spill it, doctor," I said.

"The administration knows there's no risk of transmission,

but it's harder to convince the others who use the pool. Small-minded, I know, but . . ." her hands spread out like the edge of a mushroom cloud around a burst of ignorance.

"What, they're afraid their dicks'll rot from swimming in the same water as us?"

I don't know why it is, but sometimes when I say what everyone's thinking, I get the weirdest looks.

THE FIRST GUY got it so fast, nobody had time to learn his name. I remember hearing someone weeping against the bathroom tile the third morning, and he was gone.

It shook us pretty bad. Henderson walked around for a day looking drawn and pale. "You heard him, didn't you, Allen?" he said to me. "Jesus, I didn't know."

One thing that gets old in these clinical trials is the earnestness of hearing everybody's life story over two boxes of Pizza Boli in the dorm lounge, the second night in. Like how some kids used to take summer camp so seriously, a life's mission. Bare your hearts around the campfire. After fifteen of these gigs I just want to enjoy the movies, the bowling, have some laughs, and avoid getting stung by the medical establishment. But someone started the dog and pony show. I raced through my spiel: marriage and divorce, Tony starting high school, my career in medical activism and restaurateuring.

Turns out I didn't have to punch the career line that hard. I think only two of us had jobs to go back to. Puccini was the only white collar slag among us. He'd slogged through University of Maryland courses at night, then got laid off by his accounting firm. Still married though. I figured his wife didn't know what the study was about. Mr. Lee had a government pension, a widower. Guterman, I forget his story. Henderson seemed to be going for variety—since he'd left the service, he'd done everything from meat inspector to phone solicitor for a D.C. theater.

"I don't know anything about theater," he laughed. "Then I heard the Hopkins announcement on the radio. Easy money for a couple of weeks. So now I'm here. Now I'm a clap expert."

"Use the correct term," Mr. Lee was stabbing his finger in the air, smiling. "Neisseria gonorrhoeae."

"Nah, you're both breathers," I said.

"I am not!" Henderson was suddenly on his feet, furious.

"Okay, okay," I said, palms out.

"Well if we're going to be cooped up together for two weeks," Puccini said, "I'd like to sort out what movies we're going to see, the bowling schedule, all that. So we're not arguing about it later. Maybe we should have a committee."

"Christ," Mr. Lee sighed, with a shake like Parkinson's.

Someone else groaned.

"Pooch, we *are* a committee," I said. "We're ten people going no place. We can vote on motions all day long. You want to table something?"

"First of all," he said, "it's Puccini, or Bob. Second, yes I do want to table something. Movies. I will not sit through *Godzilla* or *Dead Man Walking* just because we haven't talked about options."

"Doc Gordon did say we could choose the movies," Mr. Lee said.

"*Deep Throat.*"

"Seriously," Puccini said, his head lowered.

"I'm serious," I said.

"Okay. Let me get a pen—"

"*Mary Poppins.*"

"Hold on, hold on. Okay. *Deep Throat.*" Puccini held up a forefinger to fend off other titles. "*Mary Poppins*? Henderson, you said that? You were kidding."

"No I'm not. I love Julie Andrews."

"Yeah," I said. "Me and my chimney sweep buddies want to do her."

"You're a pig, Warner," Henderson sneered. "Isn't Doc Gordon more your type?"

"What, because she's 'old' like me?" I said.

"No, I mean, she's got that world-weary look," Henderson said. "Those sad brown eyes."

Puccini, who must be in his mid-thirties so a good referee between us, saved me from this crap. "How about *Cuckoo's Nest*?" he said.

"Kinda predictable, Pooch."

"Warner, I told you—"

"—eeni." I smiled.

"I don't want to see a film about *us*. I want escape."

"Escape! Escape!" A chant began low, then faded like a wave on the beach.

But not me. Henderson said I was a pig. He's just like my brother Sherman. Little Sherm, lost and accusing in the theater lobby when I want to see *An American Werewolf in London*. Him walking out during the shower sex scene, waggling all the seats in our row, and I had to chase after him into the street. Such a Puritan little shit.

PUCCINI was kind of a dick. Always yakking about the big accounting job he was going to get, like it mattered. Like any of us cared. Getting up at an ungodly hour to go to the gym and work out. He was leading Henderson down the primrose path,

filling his head with ideas of being Jonas Salk and all. The two
of them would come back just as I was getting out of the shower. They'd come onto the hall laughing and bragging about
numbers of reps. Kids.

Then somebody yelled down the hall that Inski was gone.
Someone had found *him* curled up in the bathroom during the
night, whimpering.

THE NEXT NIGHT I woke up in a sweat. I couldn't remember
where I was. In the darkness the room looked like a mental
ward, something about the dull hall light coming over the tran-
som. The clothes hanging off the door like somebody. Dr.
Gordon. I felt a pain, a slow, python cramp over my crotch. My
thighs were pins and needles. I lay awake like that for a long,
long time, unable to move for fear of the pain turning sharp
and real.

Next morning I caught Dr. Gordon before she reached her
office.

"Nocturnal anxiety, Allen," she said. She laughed! Then she
composed herself. "If it's gonorrhea, it'll only hurt when you
pee."

WHEN I GOT BACK to the dorm Puccini was coming down the
hall, looking simple.

"It's Henderson," he said.

"What about him?"

"I was in the gym, and Henderson came in. Then I saw he
was wiping his eyes. I asked if he was all right, and he blurts out,
'I'm pretty sure I got it. It hurt like Jesus bloody murder when
I peed this morning.' He sort of sniffled and laughed and said,
'I'm a clapper.'"

I felt my skin prickle. Suddenly, unlike all the times before, this was no paid slummy vacation. It was a lifelong affliction.

Puccini was rattled too. "Charlie said, 'It burned like fucking hell. My dick burned up to my liver.' Jesus."

THAT DAY Dr. Gordon gave Henderson a shot to neutralize the virus —somebody said it was an antibiotic cocktail —and sent him home. That was it for him.

THAT NIGHT in the bowling alley again, things were different.

"So that's how it's gonna be, eh?" Mr. Lee said, sighting over the ball. "They pick us off one by one?"

Crash down the alley.

"I can't believe Doctor Gordon would do us like that," Puccini said, writing down the old man's strike. "She seemed okay."

"You know what?" I said. "That's SOP. Every study, they soften us up with talk about partners in science, all that crap. Then they divide and conquer, like their capitalist pharmaceutical masters. Don't let the white coats fool you." It was my usual shtick, but this time I heard it coming out of my mouth fresh, and it hit me.

As he settled into his seat, the old man said, "I've been in five studies, and they've never sent anyone home that bad."

"Shit."

"We need a plan." Puccini was tapping all his fingertips together, his elbows resting on his knees.

"Right." I walked up to the bay and grabbed my trusty orange nine-pounder. Uncorked a gutter ball that sounded like thunder. I walked back and flopped down on the plastic bench.

"Who's up?"

Puccini jerked out of his funk. "I guess that's me. I was waiting for Henderson to go."

WHEN I WAS THIRTEEN and Sherman was eleven, we were sent to the same camp on a lake in upstate New York, and I nearly killed him. That's what he always said, anyway. I don't remember that part. What I remember is walking out of the cafeteria that night, the dirt path by the shore, the fireflies sparking. I said to Sherman, "You know why they do that, don't you? They want to do it."

"Do what?"

"You know, they want sex."

He didn't say anything. I said, "Think if your dick could do that. Glow like that. Pretty cool, huh?"

Because I *did* think it would be great if I could float like that in the air, send light messages in the darkness. Mine felt like it wanted to.

He claims I got the neon yellow paint and the brush and all that, but I swear I was surprised as anybody when the alkyds seeped into his skin, and the turpentine burned trying to get the paint off, and he had to go to the hospital.

"ALLEN, what's the matter? This is research, you've been here before. No one's in danger."

Dr. Gordon sounded very tight, in control. Her back was straight, her hands on either side of her on the desk.

"Right, it's nothing," I said. "At the end of the day you go home to Fells Point and your little girl," my arm shot out toward the heart-shaped frame on her desk, "and whatever else and that's fine. But Henderson's home with the clap and a fistful of antibiotics and no job."

"So you want me to give him a job, Allen?"

"My point is—my point is that this thing isn't stacked right. Not like partners."

"We're treating you as well as possible. Per your signed agreement."

I was getting no back-up from Puccini or the others. I'd have to back down sooner or later. "So that's what we can expect?"

Dr. Gordon looked at me, her mouth half open, her eyebrows slightly raised with an exasperated question.

"If you develop symptoms, you can expect the best treatment Johns Hopkins can offer. That includes antibiotics that are a lot more powerful than penicillin. If you get no symptoms, you'll return home with your honorarium and no side effects. Like you expected at the start. Now, unless there are other questions—"

"I got a question about the movies," Puccini said, leaning forward.

I didn't hear the rest, because I left the room.

"I DIDN'T REALIZE you were so upset about Henderson," Puccini said later in the gym, where I'd wandered to. "I didn't think you two had exchanged more than five words."

"Maybe not," I said. "Maybe he just reminded me of someone."

I messed around with the Universal, changed the settings at several stations.

"And I didn't think you worked out," he said.

"Well think again." I hung from the lat machine, thinking about Sherman. Stupid little shit, running away like that and never another word. I can still see him when he was eleven, standing by the lake, gaping at the fireflies.

THE MOVIE that night was *The Dirty Dozen*. I had seen it on late night t.v. too many times, but the others seemed to perk up. I didn't think I wanted to see it, so I took a walk.

It was a gray spring evening, the daffodils looked bitter for it, blown at the end of their tethers. Every footstep squashed. Passing the brick wall of the gym I half expected to see Henderson come moping out the door.

I ended up in the hall in front of Dr. Gordon's reception area. Everyone had left for the day. It wasn't hard getting in, or pulling up Henderson's file, at least the part I was looking for.

"Glen Burnie address," I said. "I told you so."

I DECIDED to see the movie after all. Lee Marvin was supposed to be the coolest, but I had a soft spot for Telly Savalas.

"Damn, he's a crazy motherfucker," Puccini hoo-hawed. Telly started shooting at everyone.

"Give me one of those," said old Mr. Lee, jabbing a finger at Telly's automatic.

And then Jim Brown, giving his all and getting shot down.

The credits were rolling. I said, "Let's go."

"Where?" Puccini said.

"Out. I got a car in the lot," I said. "We could visit Henderson."

That raised a few of the dead. "We don't know where he lives," someone said.

"Yeah we do."

WE FILED along the muddy curb of the parking lot, the blue light of the high sulfur lamps shining down on us. Telly Savalas.

"Country Squire! Warner, this your boat? It's a monster." But I could tell the old Chinaman was impressed.

Puccini whistled. "I haven't ridden in a panel-sided station wagon since I was eight," he said.

"I was a married man, I liked the security of metal," I said.

"You and Patton."

"So where we going?" Guterman said.

"Glen Burnie," I said.

"Hey, shouldn't we tell Doctor Gordon?" Puccini said.

"Hey, shouldn't she've told us a few things?" I said.

Guterman hesitated. "What if there's some escape clause," he said, clearing his throat. "What if we don't get our money because of this?"

"Guterman," Puccini said.

"Just because we didn't check the fine print? We should check—"

"Get in the car."

I pulled onto Monument, then we were gone.

WE WENT for a while in silence, looking out at the unbroken mass of dark trees beside the road, the exit ramps gliding past, the stalwart green signs with big white letters. Halfway out we got into the spirit, thinking up ways of surprising Henderson. In Glen Burnie we got lost. All the dark blocks looked the same. Finally we found it and I stopped short of the bungalow that had the right number.

"So did we decide?" Mr. Lee whispered. "What are we doing?"

Nobody answered for a minute.

"He's got a woman in there, I know it," Puccini murmured.

Then someone said, "We tie him up with a garden hose and shave his privates." Must have been Guterman.

"I don't think so," the old man whispered.

"We toss pebbles at his window and flush him out," Puccini said.

We all sat there for a moment, looking at the light in the living room. The curtains were white, and the light was a floor lamp that flared up and left a ring of white on the ceiling.

"And what do we say?" said the old man.

"Well jesus, we just say, 'How the hell are you?'"

"Right, right."

I opened my door and ran around the side of the house. I imagined Henderson inside, the walls bare, him standing in the kitchen chopping up something for spaghetti sauce. Because I guess I could hear the knife coming down steadily on a cutting board. Disciplined, steady chopping.

I knelt down and picked up a stone from the gravel around a splashblock. And tossed it up at the kitchen window.

The chopping stopped.

I hugged my back to the aluminum siding and saw a shadow move in the light rectangle on the grass. I forgot this was a prank. For a moment I imagined it was Sherman's shadow on the wet grass. I had tracked him down after all this time.

Then I heard feet on the front porch.

"Hey-hey, anybody home?" Puccini's voice.

"Pooch, what the hell—" My whisper was strangled.

"I said anybody home?"

The porch light went on, then I heard a screen door creak open.

"Puccini? What the hell?" Henderson's voice sounded muffled.

"You got any grub in there?" Puccini said.

"What are you doing here?"

"Warner wanted to burn the carbon off his spark plugs. You see his tank?" By now I was at the front corner. I could see Puccini jab his thumb toward the street.

"Did you both get clapped?" Henderson looked confused.

I leaped onto the porch and triggered a motion lamp. "No fucking way," I said. "We're slumming in this 'hood. Doc Gordon told us to go where the sun don't shine. That's how we found you."

A pebble hit the floodlamp with a clink.

"What the hell—"

"You got a *woman* in there?" I said. "Jesus, isn't she afraid you'll—"

"You're the same on the outside, aren't you, Warner?" Henderson smiled like he'd caught me. "I thought maybe you were just an asshole in there because you were penned up. But no."

"That's no way to talk about a clapper," I said, taking a step. Something whizzed past me and popped against the siding.

"What the hell? Did *all* you losers break out?" Henderson shaded his eyes to see out in the darkness.

Inside the window I saw a movement away from the couch, toward the back of the house. Longish blonde hair.

A stone pocked on the wooden steps.

"Quit throwing rocks!" he hissed.

"Hey Henderson, who ya got in there?"

"Quit throwing rocks. This is my life, not some experiment, you damn guinea pigs."

"Ooohhh," I said. "That mean you don't got any women in there for *us*?"

"You boys just better go back to the funny farm," Henderson yelled.

"You'd send us away without inviting us in?" That was Puccini.

"You come here and throw *rocks!* You can just go on back."

"But Charlie, we're clappers!" Mr. Lee stepped into the margin of the floodlamp, his hands now empty at his sides.

Henderson waved him off and turned to go inside. "That's right," he said.

"Hey, I'm sorry," I said.

The door slammed.

"Sorry!"

In the living room window we could see him stalk back to the kitchen. He brushed the floor lamp and set it wobbling, and the kitchen's saloon doors swung for five seconds after he passed through.

I looked at Puccini. "What the hell," he said.

"Let's flush him out again," I said. "Leaving it like this, it's not good."

"Forget it," Puccini said. "Let's just go."

"Just like that?"

"He's got somebody in there."

"Jesus! What the hell."

THE CAR DOORS closed like four slow shots. We all sat staring at the house, waiting. I didn't turn the key, I sat there too. The light in Henderson's window just stayed there.

"Where to now?"

Silence.

Guterman cleared his throat. "You think they'll let us back in?"

I could see Doc Gordon, looking all cool and adult, as we grovelled before her. I groaned.

"Why not?" Puccini said. "We're still infected as ever. Some of us."

We sat there for another minute or so.

"Okay," I said, "but I swear this is the last time." I turned the key.

As I merged back onto the parkway, Mr. Lee started crooning in a creaky voice. "Oh, I'm glad I'm not a breather! No sugar pills for me. Yes, I'm glad I'm not a breather. A clapper I will be!"

"What the Sam Hill is that?" I said in an Archie Bunker lilt, flicking the turn signal. "A loser's fight song?" Not that I objected. I just had to flak the old guy.

STRANGE CABBAGES

IN just ten minutes he'll be across the breakfast table from you, with his earnest milkdud eyes, effusing about cowpeas, the hope for Sri Lanka ("It's the nitrogen, you see...").

Nothing wrong with that, exactly. Except that you're here, in part, to crush his hopes. So right now just gather the calm of the hotel room around you. Sit on the rumpled bed in your boxers, and look down through the wall-sized hotel window. Try to recall the dream that has you so rattled.

Far below, two figures walk on the footpath between the rice fields. They stop. The feathers of early morning mist are dissolving—this is clear from the growing contrast between the path and their pale clothes. Soon they're distinct: a boy and a girl, dressed in the long wrappers of the Sinhalese.

The bedspread's gold fringe twirls along the floor in the breeze from the ceiling fan. *Get dressed.* You must prepare for the vice-chancellor's breakfast onslaught. Deliver the bad news and end this charade with all the grace you both can muster. As Jenny said in bed back in Delhi (just two days ago?), If you don't believe in this dependency game, then *not* feeding his hopes is the best thing to do.

But why do those two stand so still? After five minutes, your eyes are surely playing tricks—something about the distance down into the valley. And yet the lines of their feet on the rice bund, the folds of cloth, are magnified as if they were close enough to hear you breathe. Just beyond them at the edge of the field stand gangly palms, feathery albizia trees, and jackfruit as straight as muskets.

ON THE DARK wooden desk, with its copies of *What the Buddha Taught* and the Gideon Bible, the conference papers lie in two piles. In one pile sits the grant for the vice-chancellor, earnest 20-lb bond paper, innocent of the insult it brings. Why you? The boss is a bastard.

The arcs of your white shirttails sway as you step into the bathroom and spread white cream on bristling jaw and neck. Scrape it off. You brush your teeth, nose wrinkling angrily in the mirror. (Trac II, Colgate, Oral B, Mennen: all the brand names look exotic here.)

And how will you smooth things with the vice-chancellor?

Walk back to the window, toothbrush in your mouth. The two haven't moved. *Well damn them!* Who are they waiting for? Is this some kind of act? Kandy is a long way from any Tamil Tigers, supposedly. Still, it's strange.

THE FIRST odd moment came as soon as the red-eye touched down yesterday. Standing in the boxy ground transport, one hand clutching an overhead loop, you watched three people carry floppy vacuum attachments—the cleaning crew—up the steps to the empty plane. They were stopped and frisked. Their white coveralls pulsed yellow in the ghostly predawn strobes.

Your argument with Jenny drowsily replayed itself: the taxi

ride, the quick escalation to Jenny's announcement: she's going home. She was exhausted with Delhi—the loneliness, the suffocating traffic, the suffocating expats.

"Just hold on a few months," you pleaded, "we could get a new posting. We could get Bali."

"Oh Daryl," she said. "That's pathetic. You don't even believe in it anymore."

Why frisk janitors? you wondered as the transport crossed the tarmac. Then the answer: bomb squad. Who ever thought of the daily routines of civil war?

Inside the terminal, the vice-chancellor paced in gray slacks and a pale sports shirt, eyes shooting darts around the waiting area. He looked the part of a rising university official—the black hair going silver at the temples, a contrast with his lively eyes, golden teak complexion, profuse dark eyebrows.

Next to him, his driver—a small, thin man with bloodshot eyes—looked dead on his feet in the predawn fluorescence. The driver held a cardboard sign announcing you to yourself: 'Mr. Daryl Somers.'

They waited on the other side of customs. The vice-chancellor rushed to greet you. Then an hour's drive to the hilltop hotel. Kandy still dark.

Within two hours, five Land Rovers thick with scientists bounced out over a rutted path, on the way to an unsuspecting farmer's field in the hills. Sandwiched sideways in the back seat (you insisted on the back), you grew nauseous. But the driver stopped and you lost breakfast on the grass without too much loss of face.

From the rigid pattern of these conferences you knew that at the farm, someone would blare over a megaphone about tillage methods: what worked, what didn't. The vice-chancellor would interrupt with questions for everyone to consider. The farmer and her husband would look defenseless and puzzled before the circle of predatory scientists.

As it turned out, the morning's target was a village collective, a steeply cropped hillside with prickly hedges, banana plants and young citrus trees planted on terraces.

"Keep your eyes open, Daryl," the vice-chancellor said. With a fellow researcher he'd know how to joke, but you're just the funding agency's communications guy, so he's not sure. It sounded condescending.

The scientists followed him up a path. At points, they clustered to identify a species of thrip or a rill in the soil. "Erosion!" cried a pompadoured old gentleman, like a star pupil.

The technical debates raged on. You wandered across a row above the others, and stopped only once, behind a lone girl of about fifteen who stood on a high terrace in the quiet breeze. She stared down on the Land Rovers, a bundle of grasses cradled against her hip. She seemed to be marveling at the caravan, the scientists' gobbling voices, the pageantry. Her photo would be perfect for the annual report. Her back, her arm cradling the grasses—these spoke of hard times. The vista signalled hope for progress. Nice tension. The image appeared on the page in your mind.

Just as you framed her, a hand landed on your shoulder.

"So, what do you think?" boomed the vice-chancellor.

You turned. "Very impressive."

"Quite something for these slopes, eh? But we need to tease the data—yield, labor, financial return." He was ticking off his fingers. "To offer people here a better way. That's where your new computer center comes in." The vice-chancellor laughed merrily.

"Well." You remembered to laugh.

There is no good news about his request for a computer center. But there's also no need to paint him a picture of the director cackling, "Chance in hell! We give him a printer grant and some seeds."

The red eye's trance of sleeplessness seeped in. The world melted into a Dali montage with two motifs—the odd malleability of time and the bizarre nature of all speech. In a fragrant parking lot at the Tea Research Institute, an exchange between two of the Land Rover drivers floored you:

"You're shortening your life," said a man with bad skin. He held open a box of cigarettes.

The other—the dozy driver who met you at the airport a few hours before—took a cigarette. He said, "No. I'm lengthening *your* life, my friend. It's my charity to you." He grinned with the cancer stick at a jaunty angle. The first driver grunted.

The vice-chancellor approached, and they turned away with hasty nonchalance.

In this new rubbery reality, their act was like a close-up of wheat growing on the moon's tundra—in their words you saw grain heads wobbling toward each other in the lunar breeze, then apart. The moon's silence. Jenny standing in the hallway naked, wagging her finger, smiling. Saying, "You're a pastry, you are."

PACKED INTO the Rover again, you focused on the passing landscape to settle your stomach. Another beautiful, sepia-skinned woman flashed past the window, sheathed in a wet wrapper and long, thick black hair. Your sphincter tightened, as if bracing for a swim upstream, black seaweed drifting across the current, in the body of a dolphin.

Jenny again. All the things you can't say at moments when a word will ignite a fight, or regret. The past gets locked up that way, under the weight of the present.

Sandwiched against a rural sociology professor and her husband. Dr. Perera, a slight woman with a thick black braid falling over her peach sari, had eyes that started out with every sentence. She and her husband launched into an unsettling simultaneous transmission.

"It is at the household level, you see—" Dr. Perera began.

"—where the real decisions are made," said her husband.

"Yes, the *real* decisions."

Whether to stay in Delhi, or return to the States. Whether to live in a house in the Vermont woods, or pursue—

"Because you can legislate policy on high and stake off lovely demonstration farms—"

"—but how farmers actually live is very different," she said.

"*Completely* different," he said.

You tilted your head, wondering at their trick. That performance feeling.

"The Vee Cee has been slaving on this conference for months," Dr. Perera said. Vee cee, vice-chancellor.

"*Very* hard," her husband frowned.

"He likes to have everything *just* right—"

"Perhaps that's why he remains a bachelor!" the husband giggled.

"A very eligible one."

"Most eligible."

By the end of the afternoon you're once again on the brink of nausea.

That evening's opening ceremony, just 24 sleepless hours after you left Delhi, passed in a fugue state. The hotel's conference room rimmed with deep red curtains and filled with rows of metal-backed chairs. As the funding agency stooge, you sat on the daïs beside the agriculture Minister, the VC and two others. Someone set up klieg lights on one side of the room. You'd be on t.v.

Oh, to be back in Delhi, at grassy Connaught Circle on a Sunday evening! To feel Jenny laughing at your side, watching all the Indian families snapping their instamatics.

THAT EVENING, Dr. Perera began her presentation on farm household decision-making as you brushed crumbs of light yellow cake from a trouser leg. She showed great poise, and patiently constructed a picture. She showed slides of her interviewees—unsmiling men and women, poorly framed by the camera. As she concluded with the fundamental importance of household decisions, you leaned forward, lips parted, as if hearing some truth for the first time. She replied to questions afterward in rich, confident tones about rural people and their reality.

But one questioner—the older pompadoured gentleman who had championed erosion on the field trip, with a glasses-case fastened to his belt—he wouldn't relent.

"But you see—" he said. He fired off three crisp points of biophysical evidence he claimed negated Dr. Perera's conclusions. She adjusted her answer to preserve decorum. She accommodated the old pompadour.

You asked the vice-chancellor, in the next seat, who the man was.

"Dr. De Silva," the VC replied, "animal science."

"Does it ever seem," you whispered, "that science is a debate where the most convincing speaker wins?"

The VC bowed his head, as if focusing on your words. He nodded, then began to applaud. On the stage, Dr. Perera was being thanked by the session chairman.

"Yes indeed," said the VC curtly.

You instantly regretted saying anything.

SO HERE YOU ARE the next morning, still seated on the bed looking down at the two mystery figures by the field's edge. The last trail of mist dissipates behind them. What *are* they waiting for?

Put the tie on, tighten the knot.

Suddenly, the dream breaks over you: you and Jenny in a cold city. Pick up a newspaper and read in a yellow text box on Page 1 that Bob Dylan has drowned at sea. Reading the article aloud to her, you're startled by a frog in your throat. Tears blur the newsprint. You turn to her and see that she's speechless too. You both hate celebrity worship. But you can't help the grief.

"I need a drink," you say. Someone argues, with a flourish of South Asian rhetoric, that the headline actually said "*Man Drowned at Sea*," that there was no *proof* that it was Bob Dylan. You object that you read it clearly.

You feel wrung out. But the dream has also freed you somehow. It was heartfelt, as opposed to the starched obligation that dictates your movements outside this room—the need to watch your words, take notes, manage tiny grants for research on poor farmers. These have an important place, clearly. But for this one moment to be free from that, free to like what you like. At this moment, there's only the first daylight on the yellow bedspread, and its fringe, twirling along the floor.

The moment passes. *What an extravagant waste life can be!*

YOU SHOULD stop at the gift shop off the lobby, buy some postcards. Tell Jenny about the dream, a surprising aside like that could help. Maybe the front desk will have a message that the VC has been swamped by a scheduling mix-up. No breakfast meeting.

At the lobby, he bounds up the front steps in a suit and a narrow black tie. He looks dashing, the searsucker highlighting the silver at his temples.

"A good night's sleep," he says in his clipped, resonant voice, "at last?"

The two of you take a round table in the hotel's restaurant, overlooking the same landscape as the bedroom. The vice-chancellor bursts forth like a brook about educational policies that will revitalize his country's universities and youth. He's riding a wave: "—the great potential of these part-time students."

"Provided—" He lets the word hang on the tip of his forefinger while he takes a sip of coffee. The clink of china, a moment of suspense. "—that we can give them the tools. For Sri Lanka to become competitive we must have multipurpose students, let us call them. We must," he re-arranges the salt and pepper shakers and a knife on the bright tablecloth, "have curricula that can be adaptable, and equipment to support them."

It's his voice that conveys his intensity. Imagine a font of intensity somewhere. Imagine a stroll down the hill, to the lake. To the Temple of the Tooth.

"I was pleased with the idea in your speech yesterday," he says.

That brings you back, eyes reeling upward with the effort of dredging an idea from your speech.

"Exchange programs!" he prompts. "That's precisely what we need. Exchanges. The new computer center will help lay the foundation."

It's time. "That reminds me!" You bend down to your brief-case. "The director asked me to give you this." Hand him the grant. "You can sign one copy and give it back to me before I leave. No need to do it right now."

"Certainly," he says, but he immediately starts flipping pages. His lips make a flat line that shows he's seen the dollar amount. "But," he says incredulously, "there's some mistake. This is insufficient."

His mouth works the air as if you've just tossed your eggs onto his shirt. "Completely inadequate."

"But—" His look stops you. Start again: "With a printer—" It's no good. All you can do is look at him as if he will say more.

He does.

"People were being murdered," he whispers. "Two posters went up," he raises his hands in the air, "and the whole town ground to a stop. Two printed sheets. Stating they would kill us if we set foot on campus. When we went to bed at night, we didn't know what we would see in the morning. It was terrify-ing, I can assure you!"

"I can't—" you say. He's talking about the violence a year ago, you grasp that much. The Delhi papers had run something on it, passing references to intimidation, another round of bru-tal murders by the Tamil separatists in the north, but no details. Here in Kandy?

"I came to work one morning and there were fourteen human heads. In a circle around the campus pond. Like, like some kind of horrible cabbage! After that, we couldn't get to campus at all. Dr. De Silva couldn't look after his chicks. They died in the incubator. Nobody could water my cowpeas for fear of their lives—"

"Terrible."

"Yes! And what are we doing to change that landscape, Daryl?" Before you can speak, he continues, "Dr. De Silva showed me a photo of a beautiful woman. She was so *beautiful*! He said she was the one, the executioner, who sliced off the heads with one motion. They stole his sheep and slaughtered them that way. For practice!"

With his right arm, he performs a sweeping backhand.

"Where did she learn to do that?" His eyes widen.

"Very strange," you whisper.

"It showed me. That beauty is only skin deep, that it could hide her cold heart! That is why I never married! You talk of Dr. Perera—"

"No, you mustn't—" you object.

"I do not want to be *dic*tated," says the VC. "I will not be dictated!" His hand comes down on the table, probably harder than he intended. He is shaking.

"Can you tell me," you say, clearing your throat, "what those two down there are up to?" It's something Jenny would do.

"What?"

"Those two down in the valley haven't moved for thirty minutes. More."

His head swings around. He looks. You've broken his momentum.

"I have no idea." He snorts. "Is that what you've been pondering?"

"No. I just noticed—"

He cranes around once more. "Perhaps they're waiting for help." The last word ends in a puff of air.

You both look down on the scene for several seconds. The two figures, so still, they are mesmerizing.

"Daryl, please excuse me," says the vice-chancellor at last, running a hand over his hair. "This week has been... I apologize."

"Not at all."

"Well." He looks at his watch. "I'm sorry, I have one more appointment before the conference resumes."

The vice-chancellor has an excellent smile. After shaking hands, you sit down again as he negotiates the white oval tablecloths to the door. With the grant. It's like a Pontiac has been lifted off you. Check the window again, and the figures in the valley have vanished.

ERRAND

IN the century after Mt. Pinatubo blew in 1991, Bangkok
drivers shared a bond that may well be unique. For an outsider to see the motorcycles swarming at the Lumpini Park
intersection, or the circle at the Democracy Monument with
twenty-wheeled trucks charging like bull elephant ballerinas,
the overpass throbbing under their weight—these give the
impression of bedlam. You could study these deafening scenes
for months without noticing the countless signals passed from
driver to driver—the flash of a ring, a nod in the rearview.
You'd see the odd private car giving no right of way, but real
drivers like Sanit dismissed these as amateurs, outside the
order. Sooner or later they'd come to harm, Sanit would say. He
passed capsized buses without rubbernecking, not a glance.
Punctured chrome, glass shards and gray-faced motorcyclists
with missing jaws didn't move him—or any other traffic professional—except to embarrassed titters.

The shameful absurdity of thinking you could skirt the
order, how things were.

The city's explosion of roads and other measures by the
authorities had forged the drivers' order. As the number of
vehicles mushroomed in the new century, highways stacked up
on top of each other in a way that mirrored the city's hierarchy.

Key arteries rose five levels high. On an entrance ramp, a driver often had just milliseconds to detect which level suited the status of his vehicle's owner (in Sanit's case, the Governor). The examination for a license became a torturous combination of dexterity, rote memory and protocol. Mastering it required an apprenticeship. Few passed. Hanuman, at the driver's shelter, said it demanded "mind-numbing intelligence," but that's Hanuman.

BY THE TIME he banked the cruiser in front of the Parliament offices, Sanit's hands were twitching and his neck was stony from the pre-holiday onslaught. He had nearly murdered one deserving motorcyclist in an alley shortcut between two arteries. And he'd missed being destroyed himself only by a hand's width—a tanker ran a light in Klong Toei, where buses heading up-country shifted with lurching, rutting groans. The tanker's slipstream had rocked Sanit's Cruiser on its shocks.

Along the sidewalk he passed talisman vendors with their umbrellas raised against the sun. The few brown tamarind trees left beside the grassy Mall gave next to no shade. Sanit's mouth went flat with distaste as he passed the hawkers with their heads shaved, a mockery of the order.

He sped up, reached the blinding marble of the Parliament steps and crossed them in a crab-like ascent. Rolling his head from side to side, he released the iron spring of his neck and it spasmed, shooting a red flame up the back of his skull. He let the pain and heat pass. Let it pass.

Below, the Mall, still dewy in patches, made a wide base for the golden stupa in the distance. Its bell shape glimmered above the feathery tamarinds and the flat waves of buses, cars and auto-rickshaws. Its gold stirred a rare flash of awe in Sanit.

In his head, Sanit heard Durian's annoyed growl again: "How should I know *why*? The order comes from upstairs. Just do it. You know Parliament, right?" Sanit watched Durian's sloping back return to the driver's shelter. In the years he'd worked for Durian, Sanit had seen him so upset only once before. Sanit had no clue what the envelope held, or why the Governor would assign the delivery to Sanit and not Durian. It had been two years since Sanit had last made a delivery to Parliament. These things can be just a fluke of the Governor's memory, or they can mean something in the slippery hierarchy. Sanit hoped it was a fluke. He hoped he could finesse any tension with Durian by quietly leaving the envelope with a secretary, without disgracing himself, and be gone in ten.

Sanit glimpsed a guard squinting in his direction, so he hurried up the last few steps and between the columns that straddled the entrance. Covered in a mosaic of spangled glass shards with white marble behind, the columns still struck Sanit as they had when he first saw them as a boy—like a giant's pyjama-ed legs against gilt bathroom tile.

His ribcage tightened as he yanked open the heavy gilt door.

MANY WERE outraged by the changes that forged the drivers' brotherhood. Mid-level civil servants and corporate raiders staggered out of the Department of Vehicles, squinting and numb, clutching their rejection slips. But the city adapted. Demand for qualified drivers grew, and many positions went empty. Paradoxically, employers cut back in other areas, grafted chores onto drivers' positions—sometimes menial jobs; in some cases, middle management. From time to time Sanit found himself in charge of sign painting or a riverside crema-tion. But being in the Governor's service, with four other driv-ers, generally guaranteed Sanit was not overworked. He could count on at least one game a day at the chessboard behind the drivers' shelter. And the pay gave Radha and the kids a feeling of well-being.

Sanit and Radha had met on a bus—one of his few encoun-ters with public transport, back when he was a traffic cop. This was years before. His moped had sputtered dead on his way home from "his" intersection. Radha was struck by how snap-py the brown uniform looked on the man standing in the aisle. The same uniform looked sodden and shapeless on other policemen. He stood next to her seat for a long mile through monsoon traffic, fuming. When they both descended at the stop near Democracy Monument, he gallantly let her pass first. Then, standing on the pavement, she asked if he were lost—perhaps seeing how abandoned he felt, feet planted with no wheels. They both laughed. One thing led to another. They had been together 18 years now.

THE PARLIAMENT lobby yawned like a watery cave. Echoes lapped and rippled against the high dome ceiling—an icy white surface inlaid with a mural of the king surrounded by figures from all the provinces (pale northern herders, swarthy fisher-men from the south).

On account of that ceiling, Sanit had humiliated himself when he was here two years ago. In thousands of errands here, he had never let himself look up to see what the mural showed. Two years ago, he had decided to examine the ceiling long enough to describe the figures to his five-year-old. But the moment Sanit craned his head back, he felt the eyes of all the functionaries in the vast lobby register the waste of human capital. He sensed their heads cock to one side as the needle on their internal hierarch-o-meters slid as he kept gawking—from their first assessment of him as manager (his clothes and bearing) it fell quickly to underling (still gazing up like a monkey!), then riffraff. The talk had gotten back to the Governor's office. "In Parliament, of all places!" Durian fumed. "Angels of heaven!"

Actually, *that* was the first time Sanit had seen Durian upset. (They said Durian had been a hellraiser once, a snake-head's enforcer. Not hard to imagine sometimes, when he tossed darts against the back of the driver's shelter, or set leaves on fire. Or the pleasure he took in assigning cremation duty. Drivers never had to do the dirty work of erasing political rivals, but for some reason—maybe their spotless reputation, the aura of service—they ended up doing the cleanup.) That episode had curbed Sanit's curiosity. He approached the reception desk now without a glance anywhere else.

The blood-red carpet soaked up his footsteps. A clutch of doormen and guards stood yakking at the near end of the gilded counter. He made for the far end.

When he saw the receptionist's green insignia, the state of her nails and eyelashes, he summoned urgency into his voice and, trying to ignore the electric jolt of her onyx eyes, said, "I must take this to the Speaker."

Back when he started at the Governor's office, co-workers had teased Sanit about his exquisite taste ("Who's the movie star?" Hanuman had said, or "I heard the governor ask for your tailor"). As a young man, he had spent hours trailing the big-spenders on Indra Road, and would stop at a clothing store there on his way home or between errands. The remarkable fact, which the Deputy Governor's housekeeper observed every morning as Sanit arrived, was that his trousers kept their crease through the moped ride from his house across the river. Starting the car at the Deputy Governor's residence, he looked as if he had just stepped from a store's window display. Over the years, it went unspoken.

The receptionist picked up the phone and spoke in low monosyllables, her eyes on Sanit. He pressed a finger to his eyebrow to recall the location of the Speaker's office. He looked down the counter and considered various forms of address. Because getting to the next stage would require he make no mistakes. It had been so long. Why had the Governor—?

The uniforms at the other end were caught up in some tale, the women were smiling. The man speaking glanced in Sanit's direction, as if searching for storytelling props.

Someone laughed, "—because it was so *awkward*."

Sanit prepared statements for three ranks—senior guard, doorman, and clerk. He shuffled several phrases in his head.

"Is he expecting you?" the receptionist said, cupping her hand over the mouthpiece.

Sanit spoke just past her narrowed eyes: "The Speaker awaits a message from the Governor."

One of her eyebrows tremoloed and she relayed his words into the phone in a voice of cool water. She was exquisite.

Behind a blank face, Sanit again recalled the angry exchange behind the drivers' shelter just before he left. He had been at the chessboard under the tamarind tree. Hanuman had just pulled a fast one. Suddenly Durian stepped out the back door and barked, "Sanit! Get to Parliament. A delivery to the

Speaker." Sanit scoured those minutes again—the speculation on his errand (why him? what did this mean for his standing?), Durian's furious silence. As the Governor's driver, Durian was understandably put out, even though, with the holiday traffic coming, he wouldn't want the assignment. Sanit had given him a quick, deferential smile, a nod and a shrug. How had Hanuman reacted? Sanit couldn't remember.

The flicker of the receptionist's eyebrow said that she'd be discussing it later, too, probably with the Speaker's driver, who would question why *he* hadn't gotten the call. Her lower lip puckered ever so slightly. Sanit briefly imagined her grasping the counter with both hands as he stood behind her, pumping away.

Inside, Sanit's face felt starched, but he was flustered by the woman's lips and the tone of Durian's words, and he still had to work out several scenarios for the upcoming exchange. To reach the Speaker's secretary, he would have to appear impatient, but not so impatient as to make them think he was an official. On the other hand—

"This way please." The woman's hand wafted down the counter. The circle of uniforms turned to her, the laughter and smiles fading.

Her hand fell toward the older guard. "Teng, show the gentleman to the Speaker's office," she said.

"I know the way," said Sanit with a nod.

She mirrored his nod and said, "Teng will show you."

The guard, a balding man with starched maroon shoulders and back, bowed deeply. Sanit saw the weedy crown of his head.

"This way," said Teng. He turned and started down a wide corridor, his footsteps sounding like distant gunshots.

No sign of recognition. Maybe Teng didn't even remember coming to blows at the arena. But then he probably wouldn't show even if he did remember, thought Sanit. After all, this guy hadn't flinched at losing five blue notes when his man went down that night in the ring. Sanit had been sober enough to recall the third knockout, the cruelty of it, the crowd gone wild, the monstrous clanging of the ringside cage.

It was a Tuesday, Sanit and Hanuman had gone to the *muay thai* arena for the Starfeather bout because it offered good odds. Sanit's run-in with this Teng fellow happened on the way to the men's room (more like a trough of urine barely out of view of the steps). Sanit had watched the man lose over 1,000, twice in quick succession. "Nice shirt," Sanit had said as he passed. With no expression, the man turned and slapped Sanit across the face.

"Crazy," Sanit said, and let him have one back. The baldish man was drunk, or nearly drunk. Their slapfight went into the men's room, against one wall, where after some fumbling Sanit managed to end it. "That's it," he said.

"I disabled bigger men than you back in Mendon," Teng had slurred. "Smartass." Sanit just looked at him. "Go back out and lose some more money," he said. The fellow gave him a hard stare and weaved out.

Radha had been disgusted by the bruises.

Now Sanit followed him down the corridor, felt the group at the desk watching their backs. Life is strange, Sanit thought. Panels of deep yellow wood passed on either side. They approached a large, gilt doorway at the end of the corridor. To the right, a row of vermillion arches framed the sunlight as it scorched potted red flowers and long, drowsy banana leaves.

That reminded Sanit of the caladium he needed to get for Radha. She was a good woman but she got evil after his boxing nights. The questions and suspicions, smacking him as he woke bruised the next day. And again this morning. Don't forget the caladium, a peace offering.

Teng's pace continued to the end of the arches, straight to the lift. He pressed the button and turned to Sanit, arms folded. His face was wide, the color of a kiwi.

"So," said Sanit, "big holiday plans? You've got family up in Mendon, right?"

"Yes," said Teng. Still no sign. Not even puzzled. "Not going there for the holiday, though. It's no good being close to the border these days. Burma's going to blow."

Sanit nodded. The nod and his memory of the family in Mendon should count for something. Life was a matter of rebuilding and patching networks.

The lift yawned and they stepped inside.

At the fourth floor's checkpoint, Teng smiled and told Sanit to have a seat.

Sanit thought of the caladium. He remained standing.

"I just have a few minutes before the Governor needs me for another errand, thank you," he said.

It was a gamble. Either Sanit would leave with just enough time for a frenzied stop at the plant market before returning to the driver's shelter, or melonhead Teng would have him cooling his heels here for another hour and Sanit would miss the Governor's next appointment.

Melonhead glanced down at a pad on the counter. "Please take a seat," he said again.

"Thank you." Sanit remained standing.

Over the man's glare, Sanit pasted a vision of the temple garden where he would take his family for the holiday: the silk-cotton trees, the quiet of the monastery paths, his little boy's hand. Then Melonhead's face burst through, the eyes pulsing slightly. "Please, take a seat," he said again.

AFTER JUST twelve minutes (ha! he would gloat to the others later) Sanit was summoned. At the top of a tight spiral of stairs (made from the same golden jackfruit wood as the hall below), Melonhead presented Sanit to a youngish woman with a stiletto haircut and shapely hands. She was at an awfully large desk for a secretary. Sanit prepared several phrases.

"Miss Yanapol, this gentleman has a message for the Speaker," said Teng with a slight bow. "He comes straight from the Governor." He said it straight, gravely, and only Sanit could hear the sly doom in it.

This, of course, was hugely inappropriate and upset what Sanit had planned to say. Before he could set her straight, the woman's eyes dropped to the floor and she was saying, with an embarrassingly deep bow, "Pleased to be of service."

Melonhead disappeared down the stairs. Sanit searched the room for a phrase that would set things right. But the woman's eyes were still on the floor and her mouth was forming another (no doubt more embarrassing) sentence, so Sanit blurted out, "It's our joy to serve his Excellency!" This wouldn't correct her mistake about his status but it leveraged focus away from himself and raised a firewall of humility.

It was the best he could do. He felt his face burn as he struggled for something better. His shirt suddenly felt much too large, as if the long sleeves were flopping around ridiculously beyond his reach. This could mean his job, and much worse. Hanuman told a story about a cremation he was sent to handle, where he found a body in the weeds of an empty lot. It had no head, but on one finger was the ring of the order. Who would've thought a driver could incur that treatment?

"Right this way, sir," she said.

"I can leave the message with you." He swallowed, hoping his choice of pronouns, if not the tremor in his voice, would signal his true station, but goddamn Melonhead had already fouled her gauge.

"I'm sure he would like to receive it from you directly, sir," she said, her hand resting lightly on the burnished, molded handle of the door behind her. With a swift twist of her hand the door flew open and a vastness of green crushed-pile carpet lay before Sanit's feet. His floppy sleeves swayed back and forth. His cloth shoes crinkled where his toes were curling under themselves. From the far shore a man astride a massive desk beckoned him with one raised hand.

It was a swift motion, but for Sanit it seemed to hang suspended like a Hong Kong action hero's gesture.

Sanit sucked in air, stiffened his back, and imagined he was Durian. Durian could get away with this. He started across the carpet to where the Speaker waited. Sanit's peripheral vision disappeared; he fixed on the carved motifs of the desk to keep the deep green pile from swallowing him up.

He didn't breathe again until he reached the far side, actually let his fingers rest briefly on the smooth desk. He handed the envelope to the Speaker with bows that were deep but not so deep as to reveal the secretary's blunder at letting Sanit through.

On the wall behind the desk, looking down on Sanit with a face composed and compassionate, was the king. Above his red sash and the bank of medals across his chest, his majesty's eyes conveyed resignation, fortitude, and almost apology that Sanit should find himself in this position.

"Wait," said the Speaker as he ripped open the envelope. He frowned, preparing to reply on the spot—maybe to show his decisiveness. Then he changed his mind. "I'll reply later," he said.

Sanit's insides cramping, he bowed with all the grace as he could muster, and forded the carpet once more, not breathing till he gained the open door.

The edges of his vision were flickering with anopsia like fireflies. He gave a stiff parting nod to the secretary. At the bottom of the spiral stairs, alone, he sat for a moment and put his head between his knees. He tasted the first bitter drops of adrenaline on his tongue.

He managed to get out of the building before the full load hit his system and he became once more a furious, reflex-driven member of traffic.

"You've gotten *soft!*" he screamed at the windshield. In the four years since he started with the Governor, he had all but lost the resilient shell he'd acquired as a traffic cop. He cursed that melonhead Teng. He dragged his eyes back and forth, his shirt now hardened around his collar like a yoke. It rubbed against his neck with a not-unpleasant, grating sensation. A turtle's protective motion.

The queue surged forward and he was swept into the flower market at Chatuchak, a square of nine blocks surrounded by a fence. He rode the wave of cars past the furniture shops, with their overstuffed chairs, past the electric hum of the tailoring shops. When he saw the plant racks on the sidewalk ahead, he braced his legs and at an opening launched the car at a parking spot—there was no more than a half-second of sunlight on the pavement in the interval. He scanned for any orange meter-maid uniforms and dashed into the nearest shop. In moments he was out cradling a red and white caladium.

"HE'S COME, he's come, he's come," said Isara, the drivers' dispatcher, in a childish singsong from his desk. "Sanit's back!"

"That was fast," said Durian. He frowned at his watch, his tight body slouched in a chair next to Isara's desk. "The Speaker didn't ask you to stay for tea?"

"I explained I was busy," said Sanit drily. "Why aren't you playing?" He pointed to the back.

"Hanuman stole my queen and tortured me before finishing me off."

"You should've seen it, Sanit!" Isara's voice burbled. "Tut! Durian didn't have a clue!"

"Because he was tapping the table, you know how he does?" said Durian, annoyed. "I couldn't concentrate. That's his level of play."

Sanit's eyes shifted to the back door. He leaned slightly forward.

"Sanit could play through an earthquake, couldn't you?" the dispatcher said.

"What of it?" snarled Durian. "Is something up?" His voice was full of authority.

Sanit shook his head. "Don't ask *me*."

"You're the one who just rejected the Speaker's tea!" cackled Isara.

Neither driver looked at the young dispatcher. If they paid attention to a third of the things he said, that was too much encouragement.

"Anything moving?" said Sanit.

"Nothing. Not a peep."

In the pause that followed, the dispatcher and Durian stared at Sanit's white cloth shoes, silently amazed at their refusal to collect street grime.

"Go back and wait for a game," Durian said. "I'll tell you if anything comes up."

Still leaning forward slightly, Sanit looked like he was about to say something. He decided against it, started toward the back.

"Did they ask about me?" Durian said.

"They were confused," said Sanit. "I think with the holiday—"

"Bullshit," Durian said like a knife.

Just then Hanuman appeared in the back doorway. "A cheap ploy!" he yelled over his shoulder. He stopped and braced himself against the doorjamb. "Try that in a tournament! You'd pay!"

"Keep it down," Durian said.

"Sure! If he'd tried it on you, they'd be hearing it at the Palace!" Hanuman was broad-shouldered and thick-gutted, and had a face the color of bamboo. "Next time, you're down in three moves!" he barked out the door. His hands slapped together like a thunderclap.

"Hanuman," Durian said. "Let Sanit pass."

With a deep, sarcastic bow Hanuman stepped aside. "The messenger of the gods I would not delay," he singsonged.

"Wise," said Sanit.

"Just a minute," Durian called sharply.

Sanit turned around at the door.

"Don't just swish out of here because I tell Hanuman he's in your way."

There was a pause.

"I had your orders to wait for a game," said Sanit stiffly.

Durian swatted at a fly. "Go on," he said.

Sanit walked through the shade of the tamarind tree to the chess table. He craned his neck, loosening the tendons. The shade wasn't cool but it was open. A breeze rustled the highest branches.

The game was a stalemate. Sanit grew bored but didn't want to go back inside. Hanuman came out, offered the players some unhelpful suggestions, and walked over to where Sanit smoked a cigarette.

"Those things'll kill you," Hanuman said. "Here, I'll relieve you of one."

As Sanit shook one out, Hanuman said, "So, did you see her?"

Sanit said, "Who?"

"The Speaker's mistress. They say she's gorgeous. You didn't see her?"

"I didn't see anybody. Except your buddy from Mendon."

"Ha! He's a Parliament guard?"

"You said you recognized him from somewhere," Sanit said. "Wish you'd remembered where, instead of goading me to kick his butt."

Hanuman scratched his head, still smiling. "How about that? Did he remember?"

"Didn't appear to. But he put me in deep shit with the Speaker." Sanit explained what happened.

"Buddha's socks!" Hanuman cried. "She let you in to the Speaker? She's cooked. You too. You didn't let on?"

Sanit seared him with a look.

"Course not. Well, so you posed as Durian." Hanuman groaned. "You and Radha might as well go to the border for the holiday."

"Don't joke. I'm worried. With Durian getting hot under the collar, he just might call and ask what happened."

"Too bad you didn't see the Speaker's mistress." Hanuman sounded wistful. "They say she's a hot number. Course that's how it is with guys at his level. Got a dick scratcher during the day and his wife at night. Who knows? She may be a hot item too. This town." He sighed. "So where *are* you going for the holiday?"

"Hanuman, how do I keep from getting caught in the middle? The governor keeps Durian on pins and needles—he's a bastard to figure out." Sanit stubbed out the butt. "Any suggestions?"

"The beach! The sun, cold beer—"

Sanit shook his head. "Seriously, Hanuman. You could be in my shoes."

"Not likely."

"What would you do?"

Hanuman exhaled, looked sidelong at Sanit. "Seriously?"

Sanit nodded.

"Keep my head down and my hands free. Take Radha

somewhere. Look at that." Hanuman pointed, laughing, to where one of the chess players guided a black abbot through the air and knocked an ivory knight on its side. Someone tittered.

The victim frowned at the board. No comfort, Sanit thought.

"You're finished!" Hanuman sneered. "Serves you right! Playing over your head."

Sanit prepared to take a seat at the table for the next game, turned his head this way and that to release the tension in his neck, and ended up gazing at the dry tamarind branches above.

MAY DAY

SHIRLEY had perched the letter on top of the junkmail and I immediately recognized Ian's scrawl. I carried the whole pile into my den and made us drinks while she got dinner ready. I dropped in slices of lime, brought her glass to her, and took mine back to the den. For a moment I just sat there, considering the glass, the letter, my desk, the window. I picked up the paperweight geode, a souvenir from the oil visualization center folks, with 'Texaco' etched into its gray outer layer. The inside glimmered with violet crystals. Then I tore open the envelope, and heard a sound that I couldn't quite make out. It wasn't wind, but close. I listened harder and realized it was like fabric. It was the luffing of a parachute. Unfolding the letter from Ian, I knew where that sound came from—it was from that afternoon fifteen years ago, looking down from an airplane's open door onto the jagged Scottish coast, where everything was opening up.

He wrote to say he's getting married. He knows it's a long way from Houston, but he wanted to tell me, he says. His whole life has been building to that day, I can vouch for that. I wonder what she's like. His letter doesn't say, but how could it? You can't describe your fiancée anymore than you can describe yourself. So I see half the picture—Ian beaming, blinking with self-conscious good fortune, pale in front of the church, his black hair tousled by the cowlick at the crown of his head. But I can't quite see her. She's washed out, overexposed.

Yet he's talked about her, or her prototype, since we met in Scotland. From the day I parked my things in the dorm, I walked—alleys, braes leading out of town, the sands past the old stone harbor and boats leaning against the mud. Something was tugging me around every corner, teasing me, just behind the ashen house fronts of a depressed Britain. Past the trailer park west of town. I followed.

"What are you looking for?" Ian said, one hand on my shoulder to keep me from walking past him, out the dorm. His other hand twitched at the end of his arm, full of nervous energy. I just laughed. I didn't know this guy, or what he was driving at.

Mary answered. "A griffin," she said. "An imaginary beast." She was sharp, Mary.

I'd met her that first day, in the train station. Her eyes hit me. I was tired and rumpled from the Pittsburgh-Gatwick flight and the train up from London, with stale beer-and-sandwich smell still on me. Mary looked fresh, having flown straight to Prestwick and bypassed the London leg of the trip. She stood by a pile of suitcases near the street, talking with the van driver who met four of us foreigners. She turned, and I saw her brown eyes dancing as if they'd leap out of her face. They were magnetic. Her hair was long and straight and parted in the middle. Later I asked if she wanted to go for a walk.

Instead of answering Ian, I asked if he wanted to join us. We walked to Willie's chip shop. In those first days I wandered around in a raw self-awareness, resentful of my American voice and the Scots' anonymity. On the other hand Ian, with his loud New Jersey accent, seemed oblivious to the fact that he was in another country.

We were confused by the chip shop owner's tan. It was mid-October. Everyone else in the sickly fluorescent shop was yellow, but this guy stood there, bronze and laughing, folding newspaper around our codfish. We paid and sat outside against a low stone wall. Through my vinegary haze, I soaked up Mary's laughter and her dancing irises.

"That guy's hiding something," Ian said. "Nobody here smiles like that. He's not from here."

I was glad they both could skip introductory chitchat. In those days I preferred getting my information indirectly, like sonar bouncing off the ocean floor.

"You a detective, Ian?" Mary said. "You think he's just in from Colombia?"

"Could be. I'm betting Willie's a runner for the cartel. He's got that look."

"Why not the IRA?"

"More likely his wife rubbed instant tan on him," I said. "He's smiling because he's embarrassed."

"He's smiling because he just sold a load of AK-47s to Ivan," Ian said, "for a bundle. He's retailing to whoever's got the cash. Wholesale, who knows."

"Willie's secret chips." Mary laughed.

I felt better. In time I'd hear about Ian's father's business, and Mary's dreams of a clinic on the Eastern Shore, but that afternoon we had Willie's secret, and it was enough knowing they were skeptical like me.

One night after a pub crawl with Kevin, Ian's roommate from Glasgow, we climbed over the spiked fence that surrounded the town's castle ruins. Ian had too much imagination, he saw the pointed spikes driving up into his crotch. Mary told him not to worry, gave him a boost over. Looking back, I hardly recognize myself there in the castle yard, staring out at the black North Sea, part of the landscape myself. Hypnotized by the expanse of sea and Mary's blowing hair, by something pulling at me from the sea floor—dolphins, minerals, who knows.

At the Oil Visualization center now, we've got sonar maps of Texaco's North Sea Tartan field and all the nifty 3-D visualization software I could ask for. I mean you wouldn't believe. But I miss the clarity, the urgency of the *questions* we had back then. Here's this letter from Ian, it slices like a paper cut, opening up a seam of memory. I lay it on the desk and the room shifts to one side.

We were at Loch Tay, with the hillwalking club's assault there, when Ian explained his mission to me: "All I want is a woman and a house."

He kicked a stone on the dirt road, the trees were brown and naked. He gave the stone a nasty kick that sent it scudding into the grass. "That's all I want," he said. "Is that too much to ask?"

But wait, back up. I'm trying to explain Ian's quest but it's not coming out right because the world I used to live in was different from this one. The landscape was quieter. Until this letter, I had forgotten I had ever looked at the North Sea, or any sea, and seen a peaceful void.

Mary never talked to me about her boyfriend back in Columbus. She was too independent for that. Still, back in that

other world I knew you didn't get involved with someone's girlfriend, and Mary hadn't broken off with this guy. She talked to
him regularly, so their deal still held. Mary confirmed this without saying it—*because* it wasn't said. I took that as a sign that
we understood each other. We went country dancing at a *ceilidh*
or watched a movie and I tried not to get caught up by her
laughter and that shilling-sized hole high on the thigh of her
jeans, where there should have been a glimpse of panty (but
there wasn't! just nut-brown flesh). We kept things simple.
Simple and odd like two people careening around the dance
floor at a *ceilidh*.

Clean as the walk out to Brownhills. The night we found it,
the moon was a rusty sliver on the black horizon. The pub was
a half-hour walk out of town. (Kevin rebuffed our Yankee expe-
dition—he said he preferred pubs within crawling distance. But
we were drawn by the notion of an elusive, 'authentic'
Scotland.) On the way out, Ian was making Mary laugh. She
made a point about Scottish folk music and he refuted it with
an example from the Rolling Stones. I stopped and looked back
down the slope to the beach, blue-grey in the moonlight. The
houses were black spots with roofs that shone white, and when
I turned forward again I heard Ian and Mary laughing.

"This is gonna make you happy, Tony," Ian said.
"Brownhills is what you've been looking for on all your walks."

"What did that guy say?" Mary asked. "'Happiness you can
drink'?"

"That's what he said." They both looked at me, waiting for
me to laugh.

"Come on Tony, we're going to drink happiness. You're
going to drink it, then float back to town," Mary said.

"I *will*," I said.

"I will too, by God," said Ian.

Miles into the silent countryside we finally found the narrow drive and a sign saying 'Brownhills.' It took a few minutes to work up our nerve and intrude on the farm. But once we got past the big wooden door we found a roomful of sots drinking and making noise. A darts game was heating up beside the pinball machine, and the jukebox was going. No one seemed to notice us walk in.

The 90-shilling was a thick, bitter brew. I was working on my second pint when I asked Ian for an update on the quest. He had just put a coin in the jukebox. The fuzzy riff of "Satisfaction" wound upward.

"How about it, Schwartz?" I said over the noise. "Who's next on your list?"

"Don't be crude," he said. "There's no list."

"Who's next?"

"What list?" Mary said.

"Ian's list of prospects."

He looked at Mary. "No idea what he's talking about," he said.

"Yes you do," I said. "Tell us. We'll help."

"You're disgusting, Muri. What a ridiculous name—Muri! *Sounds* Scottish, but it's not."

"Just tell us who's next," I said. "After Christina."

"Fuck you. I'm not some idiot dog that just follows its prick." He wrenched his head to the side, the way he always did when he was tense.

"Ian, why the posturing?" I laughed. "It's not you."

"This stuff *really* tastes smooth," Mary said. "What do you think, Tony?"

Ian just glared. The song ended and left an irregular hammering of pinball bells.

"Okay," Ian said, "there's this woman named Jackie. She lives in your dorm, Mary."

"Jackie Tinsley? Not Jackie Tinsley. Jackie's engaged. To a guy in Dundee."

"I know. It makes me miserable." He took a swig and looked at me as he slammed the glass on the table. "Okay?" he said, eyebrows up. "Satisfied?"

I didn't know what to say.

I caught a glimpse of what I was looking for in the Fisheries Museum down the coast. That was before any talk about jumping from planes. I didn't expect it in that mousy white building on the wharf in Anstruther. It was a day trip with the American tourister contingent. Mary and I wandered up to a display of a harpoon that a whale had twisted into a corkscrew.

As I looked at it, I had the feeling that someone was standing next to me, on the side away from Mary, but when I turned there was nobody there. I looked back at the harpoon. Its furious spirals caught at my insides. I felt the wet horizon roll and water coming over the deck, steel twisting like licorice.

"Tony," Mary said. "What's wrong?"

I pointed to the harpoon. "You see this?" I said.

"Yeah?"

I rushed past her and dragged Ian away from Bernice, the Ulster woman he was dogging that day.

"What's the matter?" he said.

"You've got to see this."

"What is it?"

"It's what a whale does when you try to kill it," I said. "See?"

He was still wriggling when I let go of his coat and pointed.
"Jesus," he said.

"Pretend it's in your hands, you're out on the sea, in con-
trol. And then this huge live *monster* twists it around like *that*.
Just comes up from the bottom of the sea and spits it at you.
Isn't that it?"

"What?"

"Isn't that what we're looking for here?"

"Jesus, Tony, you're sick. You pull me away from that . . .
fine . . ." He stopped, transfixed by Bernice's ass across the
room, in front of the Wall of Remembrance. "*That's* what it is,"
he whispered.

"Sure, but try to imagine—"

He was gone, his arm was around Bernice again and they
were leaning over to read a name, one of those lost at sea.

"Mary, do you see it?" I said.

She shook her head. "It just makes me angry, all those boys
drowned so we can have Willie's fish and chips."

I stared at the harpoon again, wondering if I was crazy.

After that we gave up on expeditions for a while, until the
hike to Loch Tay with the Hillwalking Club. They seemed
hardy, independent types and talked mysteriously about
Munros. (It wasn't till later I learned that Munros were mountains over 3,000 feet high.) At least forty Yanks turned out and
overwhelmed the veteran hikers, who huddled in the back of
the coach, shooting glares at the pastel ponchos. When we
stopped for coffee the veterans made a tight circle in the gray
dawn, steaming cups in their hands, like Macbeth's witches.
The name Loch Tay sounded ominous.

Ian sulked all the way. Even Mary looked sullen, staring out the window. I sat next to her on the bus and tried to draw her out.

"There was something about Loch Tay in our Scottish History course," I said. "Some highland revenge slaughter."

Silence.

"Which probably wasn't as savage as it sounds," I continued. "Think if *we'd* spent our lives walking through gorse and fog. We'd be murderous too. This bunch is deadly and we're just riding through it on a bus."

She turned to me and her lips were moving toward a smirk.

"You *are* the same as they were," she said. "Same animal look in your eye. Walk through this place barefoot in a blanket and I'd see a real barbarian."

Her tone unnerved me. But when we got off the bus and I saw how bare the place was, I sort of liked her comparison. We started hiking, and I had the urge to shake the dew from my head and howl. Mary could put her finger on a feeling and tell me even before I felt it.

Our evenings at the folk society concerts had grown awkward. I'd walk her back to her dorm and stand a few moments in the half-halo of the outside lamp, where others would have kissed. Her man in Ohio held me back. I thought she should make the first move against that pact. She never did. We hugged, or just said goodnight, then she'd go inside and up the steps. I imagined her running up to catch the hall payphone ringing, and breathing "Hi!" to Mr. Columbus on the line. Walking back through town, I counted the sad and stoic house fronts. It's amazing I didn't spontaneously combust from frustrated desire. Instead, it left an acidic tang, a taste of how things really were in the world, I thought. After enjoying the illusion of belonging and conversation and the warm breath of Mary's skin, we shared this deeper, silent recognition on my walk back to my dorm. I thought there was something ascetic, even noble about it.

At Loch Tay, we walked together and she was mostly silent. Then all of a sudden she went off on a spiel, I couldn't see where it came from.

"You wouldn't believe how dependent he is, Tony," she said. "Lots of times he needs a kick in the butt." A sly smirk. "You know?"

I looked down, as if her words were launching out of the ground. We'd never talked about Mr. Columbus before. It was like she was starting a conversation through a wall. No intro, no name. She was trying to tell me something in a new code and I didn't know what. She waited for my response.

"You inspire him, I guess," I finally said.

She looked at me like I'd spoken Cantonese.

"No, I don't think so," she said. "I give him a kick in the butt."

I didn't ask what that meant, or what she felt for him. Anything. I was paralyzed with fear and possibility. I'd have withered if she'd said anything that meant I had a chance. A chance to lose. Her mind was too quick for me.

She sped up and I walked alone for a while. We were above the farms, but not to the treeline yet. The cold air brushed the tips of the nearby pines. It was easy to see that aloneness was the natural state. Things were alone. The grass ditch, the fence, the pines, their branches waving in solitude. They were all in the same place, but they were each alone and silent. No confusion. No murmuring voices. No baffling chemistry.

I came to where Mary had stopped and crouched by the path.

"They want to lose us," she said.

The veterans *were* far ahead, pinpricks above the treeline. Most of the pastel slickers were behind us.

"You're right," I said. "Should we wait for Ian? He looks like hell."

Below, Ian was punching the ground with a walking stick. He looked up and saw us, his mouth open, and waved his stick.

"He hasn't said a word all day. Jackie dumped him Thursday." Mary sounded irritated.

"So he's surprised?" I said.

"He's always surprised."

She stood up. Her jeans were tight and there was still that remarkable little hole scattering my faculties.

"What was he thinking?" I said.

Mary looked puzzled. "Tony, he's upset because he was rejected. Nobody likes rejection."

"He *invites* it."

We both watched Ian as he double-timed the last steps to reach us.

"They're trying to lose us, Ian," Mary said. "Something about a revenge slaughter."

"Don't blame 'em," he gasped.

We kept climbing through the rough, colorless heather. After a while, though, it seemed useless to go higher. The veterans were well out of sight, on to another Munro. We could lose ourselves following them into the snow and mist. But we couldn't go down the way we came, either—the bus had moved to another spot where the veterans were headed.

I swung my daypack to the ground and decided the knot in my stomach was hunger.

"We can't stop now," Mary said. "We'll never catch up."

I shook my head. "We'll never catch up anyway. We should just cut across the slope, take a shortcut down," I said. "We saw that path in the distance. At our pace, it's all we have time for before the bus leaves."

They both were quiet—skeptical quiet—as I tore into a sandwich.

"You make cross-country travel sound easy."

"Tony's always barging off on his own," Ian said. "Don't know about the boy. He may be trying to get *us* killed, Mary. Look at this mist."

I shrugged and ate my sandwich.

"I don't know either," Mary said. "Seems a bit off."

I looked at her. I couldn't imagine what she thought. I changed the subject.

"How long do you think those stones have been piled there?" I said. "A thousand years?"

"Cairns mark remembrance," Mary said. "Isn't that right? Where's Kevin to answer our questions about local color? Why didn't he come today?"

Ian staged a look around at the grey heather and mist. "What the hell would anyone want to remember here?" he said.

"Death," I said. "Absent loved ones."

"Heavy," Mary said.

"Isn't that it?" I said. "Can't you deal with death? It's just around the bend." I was giddy.

"Take it easy," she said.

We started walking across the slope, like I'd suggested. We

were almost to the path leading down to the road when we stumbled on the wreck of a small plane. Chunks of wing were missing, there was black graffiti sprayed on the crumpled fuselage. It looked like World War II-era RAF. Snow rested on it as naturally as it did on the heather. This wreck was *here*, where we were. With no marker or explanation, more like trash than grave. The pile of stones was more of a grave.

Ian recalled my comment about death being around the bend. "Weird," he said. I looked at him, then at Mary.

A WEEK or so later I got back to my room and found a note from Mary under the door. Did I want to go to the *ceilidh* the next night? Just her handwriting kicked up dust in my head.

"Mystic Muri." Ian was suddenly behind me in the doorway. Over his shoulder I saw Kevin in a black coat.

"Keep your coat on," Ian snapped. "We're going for a beer. If you'd gotten back earlier we were going to haul you to a depressing movie, but it's already started."

We cut through Bleeder's Alley to North Street and stopped in the Castle pub because it had a decent juke box. Ian put in 10p, and Mick Jagger bounced into "It's All Over Now."

"Women," Ian snorted. "They have a lab somewhere churning out new tortures. The question is, Where do they publish?"

"Things a little rocky with Jackie?" I said.

"What makes you think that?" Kevin said brightly.

"I send her flowers, I put an ad in the paper, and she acts like I spit in her face. No. She *refuses* to spit in my face." Ian tipped the pint glass into his mouth.

"She's married now, Ian. What did you expect?" I said.

"There ya go-o," said Kevin.

Ian nodded and held it like he was squelching a burp. "I know. But that's not it," he said. "Another pint?"

"How about if we look around the cathedral ruins?"

"After one more." He called the bartender over and ordered three more stouts. "Only dead people there anyway," he said. "They'll wait."

"I think what's needed for a proper perspective," said Kevin, "is a trip down from a personnel carrier." His fingers fluttered in the air and landed on the bar.

"What?"

"Parachutes. Skydiving. Jumping from a plane." Kevin smiled with arch mystique.

"Jesus, Kevin," Ian yawed, "I'm not that far gone."

"*Jaysus*, Ian, ya are too." Kevin punctuated this with a long swallow of beer. He said that as a kid, he'd watched the RAF jets swing low over Glasgow. He used to wave to them as they raced up the valley. He said he'd find out what they were up to one day.

The wall around the cathedral was only a couple of feet high. We stepped over it and walked toward the ruined arch at the far end of the lawn, two spires soaring on either side of it.

"Tony," Ian said, like he'd just thought of it, "how come you're not sleeping with Mary?"

I stopped. He kept on for a few steps to another grave marker.

"Don't act shocked," he said. "She's nice, you two get along. What's up?"

"That's not your business."

"I spill my guts and you say that? She asked me to find out."

"Right."

"I'm serious. She wants to know if there's something wrong with her."

Kevin moved off and made like he was inspecting gravestones.

"Ian, I don't believe Mary asked you that. Her boyfriend—"

"—a million miles away. Is he the reason?"

I hesitated. "It's a reason."

"Huh. She thought it was something with her."

This is not true, I thought, feeling my jaw tighten—Mary wouldn't discuss this with him. It would mean a world I wasn't part of. I stood there, staring at a jumble of letters on a stone marker.

Ian raised his chin. "I hear there are a shitload of ghost stories about this place. The Scots love ghost stories. Don't they, Kevin?"

"Doesn't everybody?" Kevin was several headstones away.

"One that bitch told me was—"

"Jackie?" I said.

"Yeah, she said there's this eerie young bride with a veil. She wanders around when the moon is at some phase, either full or half-full, and when she sees a young man she likes she lifts her veil and he goes crazy with desire. What do you think of that?"

"I like it," Kevin said. "Reminds me of me mum."

"Sick bastard." Ian laughed.

That story must be coloring my picture of Ian's wedding—it's probably why I can't see his bride's face, why he looks bewitched. It feels like a long time.

I'VE LEARNED a lot about people since then, learned about them the way the Grand Canyon learned about water. Every Friday I treat my staff at the center to drinks in the lounge across the street. There's an open challenge at Dark Castle, a video game there, which I've won for five months straight. (There haven't been many serious challenges lately.) Shirley, my second wife, understands me. We both know a marriage needs a little space and a lot of work.

For the space between Loch Tay and May Day, imagine six months of potatoes three times daily (fried at breakfast, boiled at noon, mashed at dinner), short, bitter days, and Sunday evenings of folk music with Mary. The regaling of the haggis in January—a midwinter revel in the cave-like town hall—stands out as a lucid moment of drunkenness between months of sleep. Bare-legged men in the dead of winter quoting poetry on the virtues of sheep's intestines. I remember gazing dumbly up at chandeliers. And then it was the night before May Day, and in three weeks I would have to stand before my father and tell him what I'd learned in a year abroad.

The Scots marked May Day with an ancient rite of swimming in the North Sea at dawn. It required a pub crawl the night before. There was Kevin, and then Ian, whom we dragged from a big powwow in Mary's room. We tried to get Mary to come too, but she was full of peeves that night, including one for me. The previous three weekends she'd been out of town visiting friends' families in Glasgow and Perth before the summer break. I almost thought she was avoiding me, but I couldn't find any reason why. We'd found a kind of balance as close friends. Ian was no help—he was working all-nighters on a final project, he said, and had no time even for a beer.

That night Kevin's girlfriend Carol begged off too. We dragged Ian, surly, from the building. Kevin kept buying drinks savagely all night, including too many rounds at a wine bar owned by two elderly sisters.

The next thing I knew my alarm clock was bleating in the darkness. My forehead and temples felt like a plaster cast not quite set. I still tasted the scotch, but I sat up and began to dress to go down to the water. Ancient rite. "Barefoot in a blanket," Mary would say.

I pounded on Kevin and Ian's door. No answer. Finally I put my lips to the lock and told them they were worthless, they were pussies if they didn't go swim in the freezing sea.

"You're fucking nuts if you think I'm going in the water," Ian said on the walk to the beach below the castle. Bright red academic gowns (another ritual) stood out against the wax-colored sand. I kept an eye out for Mary, but there were only three people huddled like drowned rats on the shore. They stood by a kind of pool, bounded on two sides by natural stone fingers that stretched into the sea. At the far end a barrier between them kept the pool filled when the tide was out.

I peeled off my shoes and socks. The cold wet sand prickled my raw feet. The other two didn't move. I felt the pull of the sea, and squelched a reflexive snarl as I pulled off the thick jacket, my sweater, jeans. By then my goosebumps were ripe and only a blind, searing fury was pumping blood in my abdomen. Kevin was taking off his shoes as I launched into the water. When I came up for my first stroke, my left side was already numb. The pool was filled with cold fire, fire danced on the water beneath the sun. I was choking when I reached the far end, Kevin was splashing to my right.

Then there are no thoughts, no sounds. I turn and see only the stark image of castle ruins high above the beach. The shore falls away beneath tiny waves, I can just make out the red gowns far away.

The next thing I know I'm rubbing myself raw with the towel as others chatter on the beach. I exhale noisily with the adrenaline of a horse after a race. Now it is spring.

When we climb the stone steps to the castle in our own cheap, red felt robes, the lawn is full of dancers 'tripping the willow' to the low-fi of a portable phonograph. Below, in the sea, a lone swimmer struggles back to shore. Maypole streamers flutter in the sunlight over the dancers. I see Mary across the lawn's broad stones, and try to dance over to her but the scotch is still with me and I reel to one side. She seems to wave but I can't hear my own words over the music and the sunlight fluttering on the streamers. Dancing around the maypole like a fool. The crowd carries two people down to the pool and throws them in the water with a roar of laughter, and the dancers disperse.

I'm turned around, and realize my stomach is feeding on acid when Kevin says, "Let's eat." We walk through town and the morning streets speak to me. The houses are stone faces with the early sun flat against them, blowing people out of their mouths like smoke rings.

In the market square, a circle of paunchy men in kilts are warming up their pipes. The cobblestones ring with shrill droning.

KEVIN SAID, "It's all just preparation for this afternoon's jump from an aeroplane." We were in Carol's flat, munching on pastries. There was a clatter of dishes, and Carol asked if we wanted coffee or tea.

"What are you yammering about, Kevin?" Ian said.

"Oh, I should say *air*plane," Kevin said. He went overboard making 'air' nasal. "We're signed up for half two at the airbase. And tell Mary. All of us."

"Where *is* Mary?" said Carol.

"I saw her at the castle," I said. "Kevin, you're brilliant."

His plan unfurled the day like a holiday flag. I remember that moment, looking from him to the pasture in the window. Cows were moving slowly toward the ridge, there were a few high clouds there, it was airy. It was the type of day when the air is inhabited.

For months Kevin's talk of parachutes had intensified. We'd see planes from the RAF base release four or five tumbling butterflies to the sky, and we nodded vaguely when Kevin said we had to do that before we left Scotland. He said retired airmen ran skydiving lessons from the base using decommissioned planes. It was a sideline his research had turned up.

The morning sped on like a freighter through ice floes, like the best mornings of childhood fleeing into the open spaces. Kevin borrowed an old cream-colored car, which was battered beyond make or model, and we rode around the countryside. The land passed away beneath us. A churchyard on a hill, a farm slope cluttered with brush, newly green. Kevin was a crotchety driver, we drifted into the oncoming lane until he jerked the wheel back.

Mary tried to get out of going. Not angry, just refused. But Kevin flushed her out of the dorm by planting his hand firmly on the car horn.

"I never said I'd do this." She plopped on the backseat. "I'm being shanghai-ed."

I turned around and was struck by how morose the three of them looked: Mary coolly distant, Ian slumped beside her, Carol staring at Mary. I didn't know what to make of it.

I turned back to the road before us. I was happy.

At the RAF base, we got forty-five minutes of instruction on how to jump and how to hit the ground. The instructor made an absurd hairless silhouette in the hangar's doorway, against the low buildings crouched behind him. He handed us blue coveralls and launched into a careful explanation. His sober precision, with the wild day set to explode behind him, made me want to laugh. Kevin looked at me across the line of our group and we both nearly burst.

The plane was some kind of personnel carrier with a large sliding panel on the side. We climbed in with the loud wind washing over us.

"I'd feel a lot better if there was more than static cling between me and the ground," Ian said when we were in the plane.

"Static *line*," Mary said, "not static cling."

"Whatever, that's not the part that worries me, it's the static part. I want a dynamic line."

There were strange pauses between them that left the rest of us out.

My butt jarred against metal as we sped toward the trees at the far end of the runway. Then the trees fell away and my stomach lifted. The horizon turned blue and I saw a scale model of the coast. It was like I'd imagined during my walks. Some crescents and squares were wider, and the jagged blond notches of the shoreline were skewed, but the gray ribbons intersected at the right points—some with little cars moving on them.

A shot of adrenaline hit me, it was as if a belief that I'd always held was being confirmed, about how the land fit together, but also about the order of things. The swells on the road to Brownhills were rhythmic and luxuriant, the trees stretched further than I had imagined. And the sea. Somehow I had known all this. This was my world.

The instructor yelled at me to move away from the opening.

"Isn't it incredible?" I said.

Carol's and Mary's faces glowed. Kevin was frowning down at the little town. Ian glanced at Mary.

"What's the matter?" I said. He jerked like he'd been bitten.

"I just don't like looking out there," he said. His face was white and his bangs were blowing around. But I knew what I saw. The floor of the plane banked.

"Brace yourself," I said.

"I've got the hiccups," he said, and hiccuped.

We were circling over Leuchars. The instructor told us to check our lines. We all started yanking on the cords clamped to a ridge in the middle of the plane. Kevin kept grimacing at the mastery it required.

I looked out the doorway. The instructor had put us in order by weight. He turned to us, the wind whipping the coveralls against his calves. "When we get in view of the field again," he said, "I'll give you the signal and you run out. That's it."

"That's it," Kevin said, stunned.

Ian was still hiccuping, Mary told him to hold his breath. Then the plane leveled off, and the airfield appeared at the open threshold.

"All right, go!"

Carol adjusted her helmet, tested her line one more time, and loped out the door.

The thwock against the underside of the plane made us all jump.

"Just her clip," the instructor said. He pulled the line in hand over hand until the clip, weightless with no Carol, came inside rattling against the floor of the plane. Kevin couldn't take his eyes off it, even after the instructor had coiled the line and put it aside.

We circled again. All I could hear was the wind and engine drone, punctuated by Ian's hiccups. The RAF guy barked, "All right, go!"

Kevin bolted grimly for the door like he was going to bring Carol back. Then came the metallic thwock against the bottom of the plane.

I was starting to feel light in my limbs, a shuddering of my body. Carol and Kevin were gone without a trace. Then Ian hiccuped again.

Mary said, "Ian, are you okay?" Above all that noise, I could hear it in her voice. I couldn't believe it, but there it was: I was sure they'd slept together.

"Hiccuping is the single biggest cause of skydiving fatalities," I said.

"Shut up," said Ian.

"People hiccup on the way down and the spasms make them flail. They catch their arms in the parachute lines."

"Tony," he pleaded.

"They hit the ground, their diaphragm's still twitching."

"Tony, don't be cruel," Mary said.

"Oh, excuse me," I said. "I wouldn't want to be cruel."

Ian hiccuped again. I took hold of his shoulders and shoved him a couple of feet toward the open door. We locked in a tight, animal crouch against the floor, my hands gripped on his shoulders, his spider frame hugging the plane at knees and elbows.

"What the fuck—" he choked.

"What the hell are you two doing?" The instructor came back and jerked Ian and me back in line by the ridge where our lines were clamped.

"I can't believe you did that," said Mary.

"How's your hiccups?" I asked.

Ian stared at the floor, gasping. "Gone," he said.

"You're welcome."

He looked at me. For two, maybe three minutes we heard just engine noise. I didn't want to know people existed. I saw water and boats and the light shifting in the shallows below. Then dishevelled stones, cathedral ruins that looked like they had been tossed around one angry afternoon a thousand years ago. I hated vividly, so I was watching my fantasy when first Mary, then Ian, jumped into the opening where the wind howled.

When my turn came my arms were shuddering again. I tested the line, my stomach churning. The instructor looked out the doorway.

"All right, go!" he yelled.

The sky filled my view, I was running onto it with a rush of air like ice skates. Then I was falling, falling like a big rock with my stomach in my throat and my legs beating convulsively against the air, finding nothing. It was a dream. I was dying.

With a flapping of fabric, the wind fell silent. Everything went calm. A brief spasm of nausea relieved my stomach. The earth grew quiet, the breeze was a distant breath. Far below, the trees and fields were hushed, the sea overwhelmed everything. This was how the world was, vivid and silent. This was home. I floated from my backpack, sinking timelessly. I didn't want to reach the ground.

PEOPLE ARE fascinating. Sometimes I can't figure out why Shirley asks for my opinion on new drapes right as I get home —like a pop quiz. Or why someone at work will give me two options on overlay parameters, knowing full well which one I'm going to choose. They're always unfolding, I'm always trying to catch up to them, still.

On the ride back from the airfield I couldn't say anything, but that evening I took a walk on the sands to release my fury. I can still see the late sunlight behind the stone tower, silhouetted, as I start away from town. The air is as crisp as it was at dawn, no one is on South Street or the sands, the sun is low over the black horizon. I take off my shoes and start across the sands along the edge of the ancient golf course. There's water on one side and the gorse on the other.

Alone on the beach I let my anger burn off and flare into the wind like the plume off a wild cat strike, my feet plying the cold sand until they went numb. There was only one person, a woman way down the beach, up to her ankles in the water and facing the sea. She had long brown hair that hung in the wind.

When I got closer I saw it was Mary.

I wanted to disappear when she turned around. She came up the beach and I thought how icy her ankles must be.

"There's something I need to tell you," she said, as if she had been waiting for me. She brushed the hair out of her face. "I wanted to tell you before you could start feeling sorry for yourself."

"Screw you," I said without conviction.

"I'm sorry you feel hurt. I've thought about how it could've been avoided. The problem is, you go back and forth between two places. What I wanted to say is you have a choice. You can either be in your world or the one where the rest of us live."

She was looking right at me as she spoke. I could tell because my eyes met hers several times when I wasn't looking at the water. She had rehearsed this.

"Thank you very much," I said.

She sighed. "Dealing with people takes a lot out of you. A lot of work. It's not always worth it, I guess."

"I suppose you've mastered it. You and Ian."

"I didn't say that."

I was pretty well deflated by then, I didn't have much anger left.

"Are you finished?" I said.

She nodded and gave me a hug. I hugged her back for a minute, ashamed it felt so good. Then I looked at her, to show I'd heard—and turned back up the beach.

It's time for dinner. Ian's letter still sits before me, folding on itself. When I wrote him about my divorce five years ago I got a return letter saying he was relieved I had gone through it, so that statistically he wouldn't have to. He had felt that kind of disaster lurking for him, he said, but after my experience he felt he could come out into the open. That he should make an effort. I took this as his awkward attempt to say we had switched roles, that I had become bolder and he gave me cred-it, even if I had fucked up.

What Mary said on the beach bothered me for a long time. (I haven't seen her in many years, although I read about her clinic in Toronto from time to time.) Sometimes I lie in bed staring up, thinking about those words, and I hear Shirley's breathing, or just my own. I think Mary was wrong about me. And she was wrong about another thing. I didn't *have* to choose. That's the great thing about this life. You keep at it long enough, you can win people over to your world.

PELAGRO

I used to like the races. My father would take me every
Saturday. These days, with casinos spreading like algae and
state lotteries screaming millions from the sides of every city
bus, a horse track sounds quaint. Back when we went to Laurel,
though, it was wild adventure. It was his only luxury, my father
said. Five nights a week he parked the red Schmitt's van
("Pipefitters since 1947") in the alley behind our house, and
came in the back door. Maybe he was ashamed of the van or he
knew my mother hated it. I guess he might have parked back
there for security reasons too, it not being his truck.

On Sundays he went along with my mother to church and
supper with her family in Bowie. Sometimes she brought a
roast, sometimes she and Grandma made supper together. On
sweltering summer afternoons, my father and grandfather
would sit on the porch while the women cooked. My grandfather, an old life insurance salesman, was a hail-fellow guy and
seemed to prefer men who could bluster like him. That wasn't
my dad. He sat there in the green rocker, stiff, leaning slightly
forward, waiting for the women to call us. It was unbearable. I
still get antsy on porches.

Saturdays were different. "This one day is for Sheldon and
me," my father told my mother. "It's father son day at Laurel." I

can still hear him, and see his silhouette against the kitchen screen door, his glasses frames as he turns to look outside.

My father would suffer almost any situation without complaining, and could make you feel weak if you did. It wasn't anything he said, it was how he didn't say it. He was a post-hippie union guy, with his Weavers records and his Kahlil Gibran. His silences could drive me crazy with confusion and anger at myself and the things I wanted: a decent stereo, a TI calculator, X-Men comics. But at the races, his nature was like a magic carpet for enjoying the whole scene. With him, the racetrack was, I don't know, the way some people love opera.

My mother's world of morning newspaper deliveries and dewy lawns always struck me as someone else's life. In my first clear memory of her, she's seated on the living room couch, looking out to the street. It was a sunny morning, definitely spring, and being four years old, I asked her about the fire hydrant on our lawn. It was a yellow metal bulb that I imagined implanted our lawn with underground tentacles. And she said, "It's for us, Shelly. It's our security blanket against fire, in case the worst happens."

When she said that, with the spring morning glowing behind her, the worst was unimaginable. Did she think that would come across to a four-year-old? Only an insurance agent's daughter would explain fire hydrants that way.

On Saturdays, my father and I would sail off in the white Impala and in twenty minutes be at Laurel, buying a program from the guy at the turnstile. While my dad soaked up the atmosphere, I'd look out over the oval to try and read the dirt, to see whether the track was fast or slow that day. I wanted the numbers, and memorized all of them—the seven-furlong chute, the home stretch (one thousand, three hundred and forty-four heart-pounding feet long)—as well as odd bits of history. Like the home-stretch duel in 1917 between Hourless, the Belmont winner, and Omar Khayyam, the Kentucky Derby champ. And the fact that Colonel Matt Winn, the guy who made the Derby famous, was Laurel general manager in 1914. Colonel Matt started with the horses when he was just 11, like me. Legend had it he watched the very first Derby as a kid inside the oval.

The shoeboard on the clubhouse wall was like that Hollywood restaurant with the impressions of movie stars in cement, except all U shaped. Banks of televisions ran tapes of yesterday's races at Saratoga and Monmouth.

"Post time in four minutes," the loudspeaker crackled.

My father pulled out a ten-dollar bill for each of us. "As far as your mother's concerned, it's five," he'd say. "Understand, Shelly?"

He'd pin crazy hopes on an Exacta or even a Trifecta, where you have to call the first-, second-, and third-place horses, in the order that they finish. It never worked.

Even stranger: it never bothered him.

We'd get in line and prepare our bets. You had to say it in the right order or you'd look like a novice: race number, amount of bet, type of bet, and the horse numbers.

My father: "Fourth race, ten-dollar superfecta, numbers eight, three, two and five."

Me: "Fourth race, five-dollar win, number nine."

I loved sitting next to my father in the orange plastic seats, passing the binocs back and forth. I'd gawp at all the seersuckers and tight jeans and polyester. Through the binocs even a guy in a tank top stretching his arm at track's edge looked inter-esting, or a jockey in white and green polka dots, or an ambu-lance waiting trackside. These things seemed to signal how the race would turn out.

Once the bets were set and the race started, the place erupt-ed. That's when the world came alive and everything that was set in concrete the rest of the time was up for grabs for a few minutes. The lazy guy in the tank top was yelling into his rolled-up program like a megaphone. An old socialite howled, "TriStar! Come on, baby!" And a guy at the upstairs bar pound-ed an iron pillar, wordless.

I felt safe beside my old man. He seemed inoculated against the fever and shakes that flared through everyone around us in the last stretch. They shook their fists and shouted. He calmly watched the horses round the turns, straight as a rod, head up, maybe lips moving slightly as he counted how many horses back his jockey trailed.

After each race, the handlers hosed down the winning horse till its torso gleamed.

"Another beautiful day," my father would say. He'd inhale big, shred the tickets and drop them into the barrel at the gate.

I only asked him about winning once, after an upset screwed my perfectly wagered win-show. As I threw my stub into the barrel I said, "Once, just once I'd like a winner. Wouldn't you?"

"Don't worry, old man," he said. "Someday."

"We've been coming to this lousy track for how long?" I said.

He nodded. "But we have fun, eh, you and me?" Which pissed me off even worse. I couldn't say why, but I was furious with him the whole way home.

At the dinner table, we told my mother about the race. "Shelly, still no bracelet for me?" she teased. "I had my heart set."

"You wouldn't believe how bad it was," I said. "I have never *seen* such a pathetic jockey. It wasn't the horse's fault."

My father laughed. "Our whole section of the stands was taken in by Slapdash," he said. "The odds just looked too good. They were too good, all right."

"Shelly," my mother pouted, "I'm crushed."

"One woman attacked that jockey afterward. She was wearing this long gown, she just ran out there and pounded him with her fists." My father waved his fists as he reached for the succotash. He told these stories as if people's anger and loss were beyond comprehension, childish tantrums.

"Oh my," my mother said. She looked alarmed, his hands flying so close to the porcelain serving dishes.

I rarely noticed the details that my father recalled—what someone wore, or their facial tics before they screamed at the t.v. screen. For me it was more important to analyze a person's loss, the risks they took.

"It didn't seem crazy," I'd say. "Four-to-one on a simple ticket. That's reasonable. But to put a hundred dollars on it, that's where you go wrong."

My father always seemed to consider what I said. "Three-to-one a good pay-off, Shelly? You think so?" he might say. Or if I said I avoided any horse with certain medication symbols by its name, he'd say, "So you mean lasix equals a doped horse with no chance. No hope. That's harsh."

My analyses wouldn't bother my mother, though. She understood.

"Next week, I promise," I told her. I loved Saturday dinners.

The summer I turned twelve, something happened that ended all that.

In June of 1971 my mother watched her father fall on his sword in an industry scandal involving a Ponzi scheme. His partner was caught swapping some clients' premiums for others' dividends, and when that guy fled, my grandfather had to take the heat. It was humiliating, and it made her cling that much more to ideas of security and the future. Her future, my father's future at Schmitt's, my future, college. The steamfitting business was relatively steady, but against looming dread it didn't hold much promise and my father wasn't worrying enough. And my prospects for the college scholarship she always talked about were uncertain. I heard no muffled voices arguing behind their bedroom door, just the clatter of silverware at the dinner table some nights. I'd hear them talking in the kitchen in even voices. I knew my mother was worried about her father. I didn't know what that meant between my parents though. And things became more tense on Saturday afternoons when my dad and I left for Laurel.

That particular Saturday marked a break in a stretch of 100-degree days, and my father had been out of sorts. He came in from the shed clutching his back, his shirt gray and damp. He collapsed into his armchair and rubbed his hand over his eyes.

"Would you be crushed if we didn't make it to the track this week, Shelly?" he said. He looked awful.

"Not if you're feeling bad," I said. We'd missed it only twice before, once because of tornadoes.

"Well," he said, "we'll see."

I changed back into my jeans, and resigned myself to walking to the Seven Eleven on Route 1 and checking the comic racks. But then my father came out of the bathroom with his hair wet and combed back.

"You're going to wear that to the track, son?" he said.

I ran back to my room and changed. We liked to look good at the track. I came back downstairs, where my father rested his hand on the newel post.

"Shelly, old man, I'm feeling lucky today," he said.

It was a strange thing for him to say. We never talked about luck, it was always about the process. I can still see him leaning back to say it, the collar of his pale sport shirt at his tan neck, the smile creeping across his face, stealthy and new. It confused me. I thought he had heard something.

We got into the Impala and he backed down the twin cement strips of driveway to the street. I waved to Mother. She turned back inside.

At the track, my father said a drink might help his back, which was even worse after sitting in the car. The second-floor bar had a view of the hazy trees to the east. My father ordered a whiskey sour. I had never seen him drink alcohol in public before. I concentrated on the program: blinkers on or off (a blinkered horse meant skittishness, poor focus, bad news), the medications list, and their past races. "Sellers. Wasn't he the one who fell off Easy Boy last year?" I asked.

We were sitting at a small black round table, three rows from the bank of windows overlooking the track.

"Shelly, how does number eight look?" my father said.

"Pelagro? Lousy," I said. He had a look that said he had already decided.

"Seven to one." I made a face. "Hasn't placed in eight races. Lasix. Blinkers."

He sipped his drink. "You sure you don't want a coke?" he said. "Sprite?"

"Eight races, Dad. Zilch."

"That's okay, son," he said. "Neither have I." He said it off-hand, nothing in his voice. But it struck me that he was answering somebody else.

"I'm looking at Four," I said. "Ghost Dancer. Four to one. Ten hands high."

"I like Pelagro," he said. "Think how he'll pay."

I remember the bartender looking over then, meeting my eye, and behind him on the other side of the bar someone moaning, "Catapult, no!"

IT'S CURIOUS, the link between your body and, for lack of a better word, your destiny. Pelagro's Lasix and blinkers—these said he was headed toward an obscure pasture, and my father must've seen that too. Back pain, an inability to get comfortable no matter how you sit, self-medication. These are warning signs.

"Put a slice of orange in that, mister." My father nodded to the bartender, then turned to me. "I see a Trifecta." He put his hands up to make a frame, like a movie director. "Eight, four, eleven."

"Trifecta? No way," I sputtered. "Ghost Dancer, okay. But Pelagro's nowhere. And eleven? You haven't even *read* about Katie's Flag." I slapped the program.

"I've got a feeling," he said. He looked dopey right then, his collar turned up on one side, his thinning hair rumpled. "Humor me," he said. "If I win, we'll get something nice for your mother."

If she had seen my father as I was seeing him now, dreamy on an impossible Trifecta...well, the two of them didn't belong to the same planet.

Our chairs scraped the mottled red-and-white tile floor. We made our way to the windows to place our bets. ("Am I straight up?" he asked, still hunched.) We got in line behind an old woman who made a simple win-place bet, it included Ghost Dancer. I took that as a good sign.

My father reached the teller and said, "Sixth race, forty dollar trifecta, numbers eight, four and eleven."

I pretended not to hear. I looked at the expressionless face behind the glass and said, "Sixth race, ten-dollar place, on number four. Ghost Dancer."

We headed toward the track, me clutching my white paper square so tight the red ink on one edge smeared like blood. I couldn't believe he'd bet so much. We sat in the plastic chairs behind the reserved boxes. He looked like a stranger to me, staring at the little t.v. sets in the boxes.

Finally I said, "Forty dollars?"

"I've got a feeling, Shelly," he said. "Don't worry, old man." He clapped a hand on my knee. "This'll be different."

The announcer called five minutes to post time. In the late sunlight everyone near us looked weird. A guy in a feather-fronted stetson with a cane stood in the aisle to my right. A girl packed into white shorts and white platforms walked beside a guy who looked like her dad, his arm around her waist.

"Change in equipment," the announcer said. "Number eleven, blinkers on."

Katie's Flag. I didn't say anything about money riding on *two* blinkered dope fiends. The tractor pulled the starting gate along the straightaway, then came the gunshot. Then everything was possible, like always.

"All right, Pelagro!" my father growled. As they rounded the first bend, the green and white jockey on number eight moved ahead.

My stomach shifted and suddenly cramped up really bad.

"Shelly, what's wrong?" I heard my father say behind me.

"Nothing."

I practically ran to the men's room, a grim fluorescent place, and sat in one of the stalls. A speaker on the wall barked that Pelagro was still strong. Ghost Dancer trailed by two lengths. Katie's Flag in third. My insides were coming out.

The guy in the next stall—an old man, it sounded like—was moaning. "Jesus, Mary and Joseph," he said. "Jesus, Mary." When the speaker said that number thirteen, Pimpernel Joe, was overtaking Katie's Flag, the sounds from the next stall changed to a low hiss. "C'mon Joe. C'mon Joey. For Papa. God*dam*mit!"

Under the stall I saw the rumpled bottoms of gray trousers.

I ran water over my hands and got out of there, reached the stands for the last turn. My father was on his feet with the others, he laughed when he saw me. "Shelly, you see what's happening?"

Craning, I saw the green helmet of Katie's Flag's jockey over the rail at the turn, then it disappeared behind the orange of Pimpernel Joe.

"C'mon, Katie's Flag!" my father yelled.

The man in the stetson shook his cane and whooped.

"Come *on*, Pelagro!" my father yelled.

"Ghost Dancer!" I cried.

Katie's Flag fell one, then two lengths behind Pimpernel Joe. But I was jumping up and down because flowing into the finish line Ghost Dancer's black streak was overtaking the streaming mane of Pelagro.

"Winner!" I screamed. "Winner!" My father barely moved, his shoulders stayed hunched. He just looked at me.

I ran to the winner's claim box. As if it might disappear! Or as if all these loser adults—the ones who couldn't crack the code—would cover it with their grease-filled bodies and hide it from a winner like me. And as I got to the head of the line and showed my ticket, I got scared that the woman would ask for proof of purchase.

She laid out the bills.

I sat down nearby and I admit, I kissed each of Andrew Jackson's twin scowling green faces. My redeemer.

My father was standing over me then, his glasses glinting with the overhead lights. His face looked drawn, the whiskey must've worn off. He looked stiff as a mannequin.

"Ready to go, Moneybags?" He tried to make it jokey, but his grin was clenched.

It startled me. I jammed the money in my pocket. We barely said a word as we passed the turnstile where he shred his tickets into the barrel, like always. The silence in the car was like some weird shared guilt.

But at the dinner table the joy came back over me as I told my mother about the odds on Ghost Dancer, the speaker in the men's room, running to the winner's box. She got excited too.

"Can you believe it?" I said. "It just goes to show, you go long enough and look things over, something's bound to stick."

"Shelly, you're my hero," she said.

My father raised his glass of iced tea— "To the first of many," he said. He and my mother clinked their glasses with mine.

"A bracelet," I promised. "Tomorrow." My mother gave my father a look I couldn't make out.

Then he told his version: how the track was damp and dangerously fast, how the woman to our left barked at the jockeys, and the stetson man waving his cane, and a horse that fell (I had missed that in my race to the winner's box), hamstrung in the last seconds, the horse that my father said would be "destroyed." Pelagro.

"They have a specially sized ambulance for the horses," he said, taking off his glasses to wipe the lenses. His bare eyes looked weak. "Did you know that?"

My mother's eyes were moist. "Jim, stop," she said, harsher than I expected. "Don't."

"It's all right, Shelly," he said, seeing my shock. "It's only natural."

Later, after I'd thought about it, I felt like my father had pulled a nasty trick. The day of the week I loved him most, it turned out, was just another chance for him to lose.

The next week I said I didn't feel so good, and didn't want to go to Laurel. We went to a movie instead. I forget what we saw. After that, we hardly ever mentioned horses.

CHILD THIEF

ABOU had to listen carefully to what the others were saying, as if they were speaking from far away instead of right there in the family compound. He knew what he had seen that afternoon in the market but that was all—the crowd, the rocks showering down on the man in the road. So that evening when his father switched off Radio Mauritania and the conversation turned to the events of the day, Abou hoped he might hear something that would make sense of those images, and the women's screams.

But the adults talked about it matter-of-factly, as if it were simply a question of who did what, not a matter of good and evil. Lying on the mat and staring up at the straw canopy, Abou could barely follow the discussion. He frowned, swatted away his little brother's pinching fingers, and concentrated harder on the jagged line where the dark straw joined the neutral sky.

"The boy said something in Peul, that's what I heard," said his older brother Mamadou. Mamadou's voice shuddered through the sepia twilight, and Abou actually *felt* the words. They made the mudbrick under him thrum like a sounding board.

"Is that why they thought he was stolen?" asked Bocar,

sprawled beside Abou on the mat. Abou sighed at the stupidity of the question.

"Yes, little fool," said their father. He leaned back against the house, sucking on his straight pipe. Mamadou sat next to him. Abou's mother sat on the edge of the platform under the canopy, a plate of uncooked rice in her lap, combing her fingers lightly through the grains, flicking out pebbles.

"Remember that time in Chengelel?" Abou's grandfather said to no one in particular. It was as if he'd just woken up. He sat in his precious old folding chair with the green-striped canvas, which he had directed Bocar on how to place so that it caught the twilight breeze from the ravine.

Abou's father nodded.

"Moors are bastards," the old man croaked. "Allah ruin them and their thievery!"

"Black Moors are just as bad," said Mamadou, expanding on his grandfather's point. "Haratins. Slaves. Moors in black skin."

"Mallik too?" said Bocar. Abou couldn't tell if Bocar was sticking up for Mallik, the Haratin farm extension agent, or trying to stir up something. Abou often stopped by Mallik's house after school. The man had some strange ways, but he wasn't anything like what Abou thought of as evil.

"All of them!" barked Mamadou. "Mallik is as attached to his old masters as the rest, *wellahi*."

"It goes back way before Mallik," Abou's grandfather explained to Bocar, in that slow voice that made Abou's skin crawl. "Hundreds of years. Back when the Moors sold gum and slaves to the whites. They would steal whole families, drive them to the ocean. But woe to them when the Hour of Doom overtakes them! Then they'll learn that each man is the hostage of his own deeds!"

Abou had never heard his grandfather quote scripture before.

What bothered Abou about the man in the market was that he had looked like other men. Someone even said he was Mallik's cousin, but Abou was sure that wasn't true. Abou had always assumed that a person with a title as hideous as "child thief" must wear it like a long ragged scar on his face. How could someone commit such a monstrous act—Abou still couldn't grasp it—and not be marked by it for all to see? Maybe like Abou's own harelip but much worse, something that marked the person as a demon, a *jinn*. (Apart from the lip, Abou was healthy, a little tall for his age. He walked very erect, as if to compensate. But he wasn't popular, which accounts for why he spent time with Mallik. Plus, Mallik was the only person in the village with a moped.) Yes, it would have to be a scar much worse than Abou's own. But the man that afternoon had looked more like a wounded animal.

It's even possible that Abou saw the child thief as he approached the market from the river before the fracas began, and failed to notice him. Abou had been absorbed in his errand for Mallik, pondering which shop would be likely to have a tire patch for the moped. And why hadn't Mallik bought a large box of patches long ago? He was mysterious that way. Mallik fascinated Abou because he was so different from Abou's father and all the other men in the village. Mallik's rooms were bare and he rarely wore embroidered *boubous*, yet he could take off to Kayedi or the capital whenever he wanted. Abou loved that moped. Even though Mallik was Haratin, he seemed free in a way that other men didn't. Working for the government didn't seem so bad, even if it was away from your family. And being the one to work with the women's vegetable coop. People said it was quite a step up for a Haratin. So Abou often found himself walking past Mallik's house to see if anything was happening, or appearing in the vegetable garden while Mallik explained a new planting procedure. Sometimes the women corrected him.

As it happened, Abou hadn't noticed anything that afternoon until he bumped into the boy running out of Diallo's shop. By then everyone had.

"He was right over there in the ravine." Abou's father shifted in his seat to point just beyond the fence. "That's where he made his stand after they chased his camel away. He faced them with the rocks coming down."

"Because the boy said something in Peul," Mamadou insisted.

"No, he didn't," said their father.

"Yes, he did," said their mother.

"Then why didn't he say anything later? When they got him and the man to the police station they asked the boy questions in Peul. First the postmaster asked, then the prefect's driver, then Mangane the schoolmaster—"

"No, the teacher," said Mamadou.

"Okay, the teacher. They all asked him questions, but he didn't say a word. Then they asked him in Arabic and he answered."

"That doesn't mean a thing," objected Abou's mother loudly. "Child thieves erase children's minds! They're devils that can twist verses of the Book, and by repeating them all the time the child forgets his own tongue, his family, everything."

"True," said Mamadou.

This struck Abou with a fresh horror. He hadn't realized that *jinn* were so cunning—to twist even the Koran to their own evil purposes! That's bold.

"He didn't steal the boy," their father said flatly. "He came to the river to wash off, then he went to the market to buy the kid sandals. If he'd stolen the boy, would he buy him sandals?"

"Wopa, you sympathize a lot with a child thief!" growled Abou's mother.

"I heard the boy walked into Diallo's shop and said, 'I am a stolen child,'" said Mamadou definitively.

Abou's mother moaned with a violent shiver. To think that in this age it could still happen, that she was not free from the fear that had dogged her mother and her grandmother! But for Abou, the savagery of child-stealing was a rumor that didn't fit in the world, or at least not in a town like M'Belé.

"The stones fell like rain," their father said distantly, as if he could still see them pelting the man, still heard the stones against the fence.

"*Vraiment*, that should have killed him," said Mamadou.

"At the gendarmerie they said his head was broken."

"They were after him with cow horns!"

"Yes, by Allah."

"His sandals are still out there," said Abou.

"I hear he's filing a complaint against the village."

"The whole village? He doesn't know this place. He names one person and we'll all come together."

"Where's he from?"

"Out in the desert north of Haïbat."

"Someone said he's related to Mallik."

"I heard that too," said Abou's mother significantly.

"Eh, Abou?" said Mamadou. "Is this child thief a cousin of your friend Mallik?"

Abou didn't say anything.

"Wasn't it last year that a child from Wodani was stolen? A herder boy. The Haratin said, 'Come with me,' and before he knew it they were far off. But they got him. Tried him in Saldé."

"Moors and Haratins—worthless!" barked Abou's grandfather.

Even after the conversation finally drifted to other subjects, Abou's thoughts kept circling back to the child thief. "Bocar, he's coming for you tonight," he whispered.

"No he's not!" groaned Bocar.

"Yes he is. He told me through the window of the gendarmerie. He said he had seen you and that you look healthier than his other boy. Your eyes are clear. He's going to escape tonight, he said. You're lucky, I almost didn't warn you. But you are my little brother—"

"Mama!" Bocar whined, "Abou said the child thief is coming for me tonight. It's not true, is it?"

"Abou!" yelled their mother, "if you say another word—one more word—I'll slap you senseless!"

So Abou kept his thoughts to himself. He wondered again how he could have missed the man in the market.

Even though Abou hadn't noticed him, the man with the boy and the camel had attracted attention when they first passed near the town's edge. By the time they entered the market from the river side, several older boys were already following him. With history the way it was, the combination of Haratin, boy, and camel was enough to make them suspicious. It fit the old stories about child thieves too closely.

After the man was singled out in the market, Abou looked for a twitching eyebrow, a pair of wringing hands. The man's hair was cut unevenly, and his face had a few deep creases. His *boubou* was a blotchy faded blue; he hitched the sleeve over his shoulder and looked around, then lowered his eyes to the ground.

But it was too late to avoid attention. The small boy had yelled something in the shop, and the man silenced him with some sharp words. Abou didn't hear what the boy had yelled—maybe it was rude—but Diallo shuffled his big graceless body to the door, a strange expression on his face. Two women selling mangoes in front were jabbing their fingers at the man and talking very fast. The boy ran to the man, new sandals slapping the ground under the small feet. The man put a hand on the boy's shoulder for a moment, then went back to lashing a package to the camel. He kept his back stubbornly to the crowd. The boy stared at Diallo, then at the mango sellers, until the man turned him around by his shoulders, and they started to leave the market.

"Slowly, there!" Diallo called after them. "Is that your son?"

The man walked on in the bright sunlight. Diallo shielded his eyes and called again. "Mister Camel-owner, whose boy is that?"

When the man still did not reply, one of the older boys said, "*Eey*? Don't you answer when someone calls you?"

The child turned around, but the man jerked the little head forward again, and gave another long pull at the camel's tether. The animal's eyes were oblivious.

By then the women had risen from their mangoes. One yelled, "The child is stolen!"

Suddenly, with a hush, the market became a single pair of eyes trained on man and boy. The old men under the canopy, who moments before had been deep in the superpower struggle, swung around. Everyone assumed a role in the chorus as if it had been rehearsed. Diallo, the solo, lumbered into the sunlight from the stoop in front of his shop. He raised his hand, gray with flour, to hail the man with the camel.

"I just want to hear the boy say you are his father," he said. The man continued to retreat. "Does the boy speak your language or ours?"

"He speaks his father's tongue!" said the man in a guttural accent of the Arabic from the north. "Every stranger, does he have to prove he is father?"

Abou could see the man's hand on the boy's shoulder, it was shaking.

"Not everyone, friend," said Diallo. "But I want to hear your boy say it, since he just said something else in my shop."

The man frowned. "What did he say?"

But it wasn't necessary to hear the words. Like Abou, everyone saw all they needed to in the man's look, in the hand on the boy's shoulder, in the child's face. The child said nothing. What more proof was needed? Centuries of fear in those eyes.

As the first small stones began to fly, a woman swooped down on the boy and pulled him from the child thief's grasp. The man lunged after her, caught the hem of her *boubou*, but then pulled himself up. In that moment, the camel sidestepped between him and the flying rocks. A stone caught it in the neck and it bolted. The man flailed at the animal's neck as if to ride. The boys who were closest reeled back as the camel bellowed, its eyes strangely bored above the powerful legs. It scattered people in all directions, then dashed across the road and bounded out of town. The boys took off after the man, who lurched, scraped and bleeding, toward the ravine.

LATE THAT NIGHT, Abou dreamt he was taking the ablutions kettle to the latrine when the man in the faded blue *boubou* stepped from behind a corner. His face looked different now—it took a second for Abou to realize it was Mallik's face—and his voice was garbled horribly, but just recognizable. Abou stumbled back against the wall, unable to cry out to his parents, though he could hear their calm voices on the other side of the wall. The man grabbed Abou's arm and somehow, with his strange sounds and his wild hair, uttered a demand. He needed Abou to give him something, maybe time to escape. The man's face was expressionless but with an awful intense gaze. He implored Abou, threatened him, so Abou knew his life depended on his promise. Abou couldn't think, or talk, or tell himself it was a dream.

Something flew over the compound and exploded against the wall beside him in a cloud of mud plaster dust. A rock. Then came another. Abou covered his head, defending himself from the blind missiles that battered them both. Then he was lying in the darkness, with Bocar snoring on the mat next to him.

The pale sunlight on the threshold was reassuring. He heard the sounds of the cook-fire outside and his mother's voice chiding his sister.

Abou rose, took the ablutions kettle and went outside to wash the night from his face.

After breakfast he walked in the direction of Mallik's house, thinking that he was just wandering. It was still early. He passed a woman walking to the market with a gourd of milk on her head. He thought about how Mallik always managed to buy tea for guests, and about all his rides to Kayedi. Was all that on a government salary? Abou's stomach churned as he neared Mallik's house.

Through the open door he saw Mallik hunched over some papers at his small table. Abou turned into the compound quickly at the last moment, as if he hadn't decided until just then to visit Mallik. When he reached the doorway, he saw that Mallik was grumpy and disheveled.

"Did you wake with peace?" The man spat the greeting. Sometimes his harsh accent could make Abou laugh.

"*Jam tan*," Abou replied.

"I have a headache," said Mallik. "This town gives me a headache. Sit."

Abou lowered himself onto the edge of the mat on the floor. Mallik stood and went to the water jug. He drew a cupful and drank it in one draught while Abou stared at the sweating ceramic, the patterns of moisture on the clay pot's bulging sides. Mallik offered the cup to Abou.

"Abou, don't be like Diallo the shopkeeper."

Abou glanced over the cup's rim at the man with a tightening of his throat. Mallik's face was expectant, commanding, like the face in Abou's dream. What was he asking?

"What about Diallo?"

"I have had credit at his shop since I came to M'Belé," said Mallik. "Three years. This morning I go to buy bread, and he wouldn't sell me a loaf because I was five francs short. Five francs! I said, 'Diallo, you've given me five *thousand* francs in credit before, and I repaid you on time. Today you begrudge me five francs?' I had to walk back here and send a boy with the money to get bread, and by then there were just burnt loaves left. Hard as rock." Mallik knocked the butt of one against the table. "How's your brother?"

"What?" said Abou, startled again.

"The other day you said Bocar's foot was infected." Mallik sat down and picked up his papers. "I told you to get disinfectant at the dispensary, but you forgot to tell your mother, didn't you?" he said with irritation.

"He's better," said Abou. "But not completely well," he added quickly. Mallik's interest in Bocar's health alarmed him. The morning sunlight, so reassuring at home, looked stupid and indifferent on Mallik's sloping threshold. Abou's throat was dry again.

"It will go on for days if he doesn't keep it clean."

"Mallik, did you hear about the man yesterday?" Abou blurted out. His voice echoed in the hollow room.

"What man?"

"The man with the boy who—"

"You mean the wretch they nearly killed?" Mallik snorted. "I heard about it. Pathetic. It took hours to catch his camel. When they found it it was eating melons in Jeynaba Diop's bottomland. And what the boy suffered!"

Abou still couldn't tell which side Mallik was on. "Mallik," he said, "you're not a cousin of the child thief, are you?"

Mallik stopped shuffling his papers and looked down on the boy, the whites of his eyes growing like coals in a breeze. He sat in his chair above Abou, with the dark ceiling high above his glowering face.

"Yes!" hissed Mallik. "Same grandparents! Of course! All of us Haratins are. We steal children together and share the profits. We're all devils!"

Abou felt the blood racing in his neck. He looked down at the patterns of color swirling on the mat. Twice he glanced up and Mallik was still glaring.

"One day we'll get *you*!"

Mallik's mocking tone stung him with fear and humiliation. Fear that what Mallik was saying was true, humiliation that it was a cruel joke.

Mallik shoved the table from him. It teetered for an instant, then overturned with a crash, scattering papers and the unlit lamp.

"Look at that! Abou, don't be like Diallo and the others!" he commanded. "You cannot afford it. We cannot—" he broke off. He stared at the floor, at the threshold where the lamp had rolled to a stop. The muscles of his jaw moved slowly, like a fish's gills. "Help me clean this up."

After a minute, Mallik said more quietly, "Abou, you heard what happened, right? At the gendarmerie?"

Abou said nothing.

"They took them both there, the man and the boy. They locked up the man, his head still bleeding. I heard that one of the guards tossed him an oily rag for the wound. And they took the boy into the office and sat him down. This frightened little boy. His feet didn't reach the floor. They took turns asking who his father was. In Wolof. In Pulaar. In Soninké. They really thought they were helping the boy. But he wouldn't answer. Finally, they asked him in Arabic. Finally they let *me* ask him.

'Who is your father?' I said. And he said very clearly, 'The man in the cage.'

"They let them go this morning, Abou. The man was the boy's father."

This struck Abou as odd. He watched Mallik for further signs, but didn't see any. Hard to tell. He believed that Mallik wasn't related to the man. But what about the *jinn* that his mother had talked about – did the man in jail have any power at all? What about real child thieves and how they worked? And how could so many people multiply a mistake and it still be wrong? Abou didn't understand and he wasn't sure that Mallik did either.

SAIGON HAIRCUT

GETTING a decent haircut is so hard for me that when I find a barber who can do the job, I go to lengths. Hainie tried for the first year we were together, but one really bad episode made us both realize I should get someone else to master my steel wool.

For a while I went to Ursula, a dark Salvadoran woman, and she did an okay job. I was willing to sit waiting a half hour beyond my appointment time, because she put a lot more intelligence into it than others in the shop, and besides I couldn't talk with them. Ursula got it right: short across the back and sides, a little longer on top, weeded in a way that didn't make the whole mass stick straight up after two weeks.

I was the only gringo there most times, sitting quiet in my chair watching a day-time talk show on the Latino channel, not getting a word of it. Conversations swirling around me.

Late that spring the shop where I worked got word that we'd lost the big Carr contract, and that about half of us would be let go. Carr had decided to go with a bootstrap outfit that could get flowers on the cheap to wherever. I heard the rumor one evening, and the next afternoon I got sacked. It took me a few beers to get up the nerve to tell Hainie.

"You'll find something," she said. "I have faith."

Then we moved out of that neighborhood to a place with lower rent, and it was a severe pain to go to Ursula for my haircuts. It was hell in our new place. I tried the stylist at the edge of the nearest commercial strip, and came out looking like Eddie Rabbitt.

"You look like Eddie Rabbitt," Hainie said.

"Kid me not."

"I'll do your hair next time." She turned to open the fridge so I wouldn't see her smirk.

Three weeks later I tried Wilson Boulevard Haircutters, in another strip. I smiled to the two Asian cutters as the bell went jingling, took my seat beside a stack of *People*. On the wall behind each barber's chair, above the mirrors, was the barber's name in black and gold mailbox letters. The woman under the one labeled 'Cindy' shook out her apron and nodded to me.

"Ohh, your hair so thick!" she said when she started. I smiled. She didn't say it was steel wool, or troublesome.

I felt the ridges of the electric clippers excavate the back of my skull. The upward strokes carved out a new shape there. Not that brutal, I guess. It's what we come in for. To get refinished, made new and improved like the guys in the head shots on the wall. And that requires some rough treatment. Each time, I hope, it'll be better. Which is why nothing humiliates me as much as a bad haircut.

The bell on the doorchain jingled and I saw a gawky teenager enter wearing long shorts. He said hi nervously and dropped into a chair.

Cindy kept at it with the electric clippers.

I got home and Hainie said, "Jesus, she really did you. I don't recognize you."

It was true. I had never seen the outline of my skull so clearly. Cindy had buzzed me down to a level beneath my personality, to where I was a businessman or Nazi or something. It was a shock. My face looked shrewder than before. I turned to see the other side in the hall mirror. At least I didn't look like Eddie Rabbitt.

A couple of days later I went to interview for a new job. I planned to talk this guy into letting me do the plants at his mall, the same one where Hainie found a job at a daycare outfit. At my old job I had spent the slack time between deliveries with the horticulturist, and picked up enough of the lingo to feel like I knew something. But sitting in the mall guy's office I suddenly sensed that would go nowhere, and I switched tacks.

"Your marketing department needs beefing up," I said. "I can help you out."

He was taken aback, an older guy used to dealing with people on what they'd phoned him about—mall maintenance, leasing, janitorial services, security. Plants. He seemed to pause before the new, shrewd me.

"What did you have in mind?" he said.

I painted an aggressive plan for positioning the mall differently. Not as a hangout for teenagers and exercise walkers, but a trendy pull for after-dinner professionals. Put in a few bars across from the multiplex. Extend the hours to 10 p.m. or later. He clacked the stainless-steel balls suspended on his desk, clack-clack, and said he'd talk it over with his colleagues, thank you very much. I felt it would be confusing to bring up plants after that, so I thanked him back and said I'd be in touch.

I got in my car and looked in the rearview, touched the spot above my ear where Cindy had edged a clean curve of skin down to my neck. I drove to the library and checked out five books on management and advertising, and one on bookkeeping, realizing I was overdue on getting a handle on double entry.

Hainie took one look at the stack of books on the kitchen formica and said, "Woo-hoo! Someone robbed the bookmobile."

"It's an investment," I said.

"So," she said, picking one up. "Mall Maintenance for the Millennium?"

"So?" I said.

The next week I called the guy back about the marketing position. He said they were interested in some of my ideas, but he had to talk it over with his boss. Could I call back the following week? "Sure, talk it over," I said.

Not to have all my eggs in one basket, I called up the shopping strip where Wilson Boulevard Haircutters was located. Just wanted some information, I said, but as I spoke with the strip manager I salted the conversation with a couple of my ideas. For instance, that the strip might take advantage of being so close to the court house by putting in a small notary booth just off the management office, maybe with fax and xerox service. Key duplication, that sort of thing. I played out the scenario a bit with the woman on the phone so she could catch the vision—the name change ("Court House Place"), the theme. I lost some steam when her call-waiting clicked and she let me cool on the line for five minutes, twice. But when she came back on she said she'd let me know when she'd had a chance to think about it.

After dinner that night Hainie told me about the craziness

at the daycare, the flu was wreaking havoc with the kids but her boss wouldn't send the disease vectors home. I got distracted, though, following my new ideas around the block. I picked up the advertising book from the library but couldn't focus. I ended up flipping through the pages, looking at the charts and pictures of sample posters.

IN BED that night I decided it was time for another haircut. It had been ten days, I was starting to look a little fuggy over the ears and thought maybe I could follow up with the strip manager afterward. Nothing seemed to be happening with the mall guy, and I'd probably need the haircut to launch the appointment I'd made with a department store that Friday.

"So you think we should have a kid?" I said, staring up at the ceiling.

"Not tonight," she said. "Not after today. They're vectors."

I went into the barber shop the next day at lunch time, but when I walked in I saw that Cindy wasn't there. I asked when she'd be back.

"Cindy take holiday with her parents," the woman said. "At the beach. Have a seat."

I said no, I'd come back. Just tell me when Cindy will get back from the beach.

"I don't know," the woman said. "Please, take a seat." The letters on the wall over her chair spelled 'Tronh'. She was older than Cindy, and her grown-out perm looked more hardbitten.

I grumbled and thumbed through *People*. "How about if I come back next Tuesday?" I said.

"It's okay," she said, blowdrying the last hairs off the marine in the chair, "I'll take care of you now."

Boy did she. The ham-handed bitch was on the phone most of the time she sheared me, yammering in her language instead of paying attention to my head. I watched it all in the mirror across the shop, like a bad dream. I came out of the shop looking like a Parris Island reject. Walked straight past the strip manager's office, too humiliated to go in.

"That's the thing about a haircut," Hainie said when I came in that afternoon late, "you can't undo it."

"Thank you, Heloise," I said. "I was going to see one of my prospects tomorrow."

"Relax," she said. "Buzz cuts are back. Dress artsy."

"This ain't artsy," I said, pointing to my head.

She went back to her magazine. "I thought you liked the close cut now?"

"Not like *this*," I said. "This has no, no style. You must be able to see that."

"Don't sweat it, Sweetie." She winked, but I looked away. "Skinhead's not as bad as it used to be."

I changed into jeans and went out for a walk.

Since I didn't have anything going that afternoon, it was a long walk. The nerves on my scalp kept going off like flares and every breeze that came down the road made my whole head tingle. I passed the plywood frames of a new development going up on the right, the lawns turned into mud soup under the dozers. Probably just the fact that the dozer was sitting there unmanned made the place inviting, like an open medicine cabinet. I hopped the trench around the foundation.

The sound of my footsteps on the subflooring brought back the feel of sneaking through construction sites as a teenager. I looked at the electrical boxes and wires in the wall frames, the aluminum ductwork. Tried to find a new way into it, an idea I could use. But all that came was anger, my head shorn by someone who couldn't be bothered to get off the phone.

I picked up a leftover two-by-four and tossed it out the space for a window. If there'd been drywall, I would've punched a hole in it.

Then I heard a noise down below. I walked over to the staircase risers and looked down. In the small square that would later be a bathroom, a guy in coveralls was pulling at a roll of copper tubing. Yanking it from the floor, and rolling it up.

"What are you doing?" I yelled.

When he looked up, I could see a round face under his baseball cap, scared eyes.

"I'll split it with you," he said. "I don't want trouble. There's enough."

What the hell would I want with a bunch of hot copper? By the time I got down the steps he was talking fast. "We can sell it to my brother-in-law. His company's building these shitholes in the first place. They'll buy back this stuff and no one'll be the wiser. They're always looking to buy seconds—dishwashers, pipe. No questions asked."

The guy's cheeks were waggling, his boxer eyes were darting all over the place like he was finding castoff dishwashers in every corner. He didn't look like a promising business partner.

"I usually work alone," I said.

"Sure, sure," he said. "Take forty percent, do whatever the hell you want." His hands fluttered like pink birds.

"That your truck out there?" I said, turning toward the front.

He wiped his forehead, nodded reluctantly.

"I don't want trouble from you guys," he said. "Last time you screwed me good. Without even talking to me, or trying to work something out. Didn't appreciate that, man."

"What are you talking about?"

"You skinheads are like, the weasliest fuckers." He laughed again, nervously, maybe realizing his social skills weren't up for this kind of exchange. "No offense. But you think I don't make a connection between my last load getting freaked and you coming by now? You think I'm eff-ing dense? I'm not that dense."

His hands kept working the air.

I said, "So how do I know your brother-in-law deals you square?"

HAINIE took a look at the loot in the garage that we share with the other renters and whistled. "You drive a hard bargain," she said. She seemed nervous, the way her eyes darted over all the rolls of copper.

"I'm no patsy witness," I said, and gave my head a rub.

She said, "Yeah?" Then she kissed me. "I hope you're not doing this for me.

We went inside. After we'd made love and I was drifting off to sleep, I saw myself in a dim light with a wild bush of dark hair, and half a moustache. I remember thinking, Who the hell is *that*?

I was at the desk in the living room with my solar-powered calculator the next morning, still figuring an acceptable margin, when the police came to the door. I saw the badge through the peephole and said, oh shit.

He asked some questions and left, but he was back later

with a warrant and by the next day, I was looking at the possibility of time. I was charged and a preliminary hearing was set for three weeks later. I don't remember hearing any gavel, just Hainie looking at me, blinking away tears.

I swore off haircuts for a while. Didn't do anything for a few days. I almost went back to the barber shop to tell Tronh what she'd done to my life. I got to the strip mall and was nearly at the door, ready to hear the tinkle of that goddamn little bell, ready to send a stack of magazines flying with my foot, when I caught my reflection in the window of a Hallmark store.

I scared myself. I stopped there on the sidewalk, looked both ways to the end of the strip. What the hell led me to a barber shop for revenge?

I stood staring at the shamrocks and St. Patrick's Day cards in the window for a long time. Just breathing. Remembered Hainie's birthday. Told myself I needed to get back on the runaway horse of life, go home and change clothes, try again with the mall manager. Take things one step at a time in the weeks before the hearing.

So I walked home, put on khakis and a blue shirt, my sportcoat. Felt like an impostor, looking in the mirror. Then I said, "Good to see you again, sport," and smiled like I meant it.

But it took ten days to get up the nerve to go back to the mall, and the operations manager's office.

"So," I said, "did you decide on extending the hours? A TGI Friday's for the empty slot across from the theaters?" I laughed as if picking up a conversation we'd had the day before.

He gave the steel balls on his desk a flick. "You know, we did talk about that," he said. "No action yet, but my boss was intrigued. We might catch him right now, in fact. Can you wait here a second?"

He went down the hall and I glanced at his shelves—directories, mostly. Several minutes went by, then I turned and saw him and another man pass the doorway, headed out toward the food court, so I stood and said, "Hi!" They stopped and I got introduced to Harold Quay, the mall supervisor, a hearty guy with a ten-pin paunch coming out of his dark suit jacket. We shook hands.

"How ya doing?" he said. "Jim tells me you got ideas. Sounds like we should explore some."

"When's a good time?" I said.

He laughed. "Not today," he said, "I got a grand opening in five minutes. You got a card?"

I said I'd left them all in my other jacket, but I could write down my phone number and pager number. I quickly made up the second one. (If he tried it, I'd say later, "That damned network!" How many times had I heard people say that?)

"The end of the week I often have some work near here," I said. "Maybe we could set something up for then."

"Could be, could be," Harold said. "I'll check my schedule and give you a call."

Which meant I'd go until the end of the week, at least, with no work, no clear idea how I'd present myself at the hearing.

I got home and took off my coat and tie, parked myself on the couch. Hainie wouldn't be home for another hour or so. I took off my shoes, picked up a magazine but couldn't focus on reading, so I turned on the t.v. I felt like a complete sham, like an actor without anything left underneath. I mean, I'd tried to turn every part of me outward at one point or another to see which ones worked. What was left? Hainie would give me her smile and say, "You just need a good influence. We'll get through this." Like I was one of her daycare kids. I turned the t.v. off, looked out the window. A school bus stopped and a lone kid got off. He walked down the street, kicking a stone.

I'll get through this, I told myself.

I decided to make a special dinner for Hainie: a turkey stew I hadn't made in years, since we first moved in together. I checked the fridge, made a list of what I'd need. I didn't feel like facing the commuter rush at Shopper's Warehouse, so I walked to the Asian market in the strip mall three blocks away. I was walking down the aisle toward the butcher's counter in back, when who should I see but Cindy, from the barber shop! I ran to catch up with her.

"You're back," I said.

"I never went away," she said.

"But I went to the shop last week and Tronh said—"

"Oh, that woman! She *evil*," she said, wrinkling her nose. "We disagree too much, so I went to work at another shop. With a partner."

"Where?" I said. I nearly grabbed her wrist.

"MacArthur Boulevard. You come there and I'll give you really good haircut. Like last time."

"Great. Next week?"

"Sure," she said, glancing at my hair with a moment's hesitation, probably seeing that it was too soon for a cut. I was so glad to see her I left the shop without the turkey. I didn't realize it until I got home, so we had a veggie stew that night. Hainie was sweet, and said it was delicious.

The next morning I couldn't wait, I drove up MacArthur Boulevard, looking on both sides of the street through the quiet neighborhood for the striped barber pole. I parked the car and walked past the shop twice before walking inside.

Cindy looked up from the head she was doing as the bell went off and smiled. "Why hello!" she said. She introduced me to her partner, also Vietnamese.

"I'll be out of town next week," I said quickly. "So I decided, what the heck, I'll come today."

"Okay, good," she said with each syllable open and unstressed, letting the last one trail off. "Please, have a seat."

I thumbed through another issue of *People*, glancing at Leo DiCaprio and admiring Minnie Driver, mulling over opening arguments in my head. "Your honor, it's plain to see that I'm..." I got stuck. I felt sure my appearance would speak for itself, but what if I had to articulate it? What was I aiming for? Smart, successful. I didn't see it in *People*, or in the headshots framed on the walls above the barber shop mirrors (the models looked successful, but stupid). I didn't even see it in Hainie's eyes when she looked at me lately. I corrected myself: of course that was wrong. Hainie was the only one who believed in me.

"Okay," Cindy said, as she shook out the apron. "What would you like?"

"Like last time," I said.

"Right," she said, and got started. She asked me if I was working that day.

"No," I said, "I'm off this afternoon."

She nodded at me in the mirror opposite and kept at it with the electric clippers. She didn't even have to use the comb, it was still so short from last time. She finished with the sides and started on the top. I noticed gray in the brown clumps on the apron like sawdust. I was in good hands. My head dropped forward, I stared at the green mat in front of three waiting chairs. The comb against my scalp, the snipping sound. Irritating sensations, so close to the ears and nerves, the tightness at the collar where the red apron is clipped in place, the splinters of hair against my neck. Yet I could relax.

Then the shaving cream behind the ears. The straight blade comes out—downward strokes in front of my right ear, then she carves a line over the ear, holds it forward to scrape a line behind. The skk-skk noise doesn't sound like my head, sounds like sandpaper. Then she wipes off the back of my neck, wets her hands and gives me a little neck massage as she cleans it off.

I glanced up into the endless series of mirrors on the opposite wall. Cindy met my gaze there.

"Nice," she said with a smile.

She brushed the little hairs off my neck and collar, hit me with the vacuum hose for good measure.

"Good haircut," I said.

"Good head," she said, laughing. She patted the back of my head. "You can be my model." I love that twinge of embarrassment, like a shy kid basking in her glow. The flirting, the feeling of air on my scalp. Cindy's years older than me, you can see her laugh lines. I tipped her five bucks, more than I could afford. I was ready for the world, new for another couple of weeks.

She shook out the apron. "Have a good day!"

"You too!" I said, sounding more jolly than I ever do. What I needed was to come in here every week. Outside I checked my reflection in the window. I felt ready for the mall manager.

I decided to stop by the daycare first and test the look on Hainie before I went to the mall office. The daycare was on the mezzanine level, and the mall manager's office was above it—you could almost see it from the daycare entrance, at the top of the escalator. I didn't necessarily want the manager to know my wife worked at one of his leases, so I slipped in as a dose of five kids launched out the double doors, two mothers trailing behind. I found Hainie straightening up the main playroom, which was strewn with big, bold-colored legos and sleep mats.

"Well look at you," she said, "You got a haircut."

"What do you think?" I said. "Good enough to keep me out of jail?"

Just then Harold Quay, the mall guy came through the door, a four-year-old clutching his right hand.

"Don't know," Hainie said, "but probably good enough to get you laid—"

"Hello!" I blurted, looking past her.

"It's you," he said. "And… jail?"

"Just a joke," I said. "Some market research."

Hainie ducked her chin into her neck.

"Really? Your initiative is refreshing." The guy looked down at his kid. "Chloe, this man wants to work for Daddy."

The girl squinted at me. "He doesn't have any hair," she said.

"I find that parents with children here," I continued, freestyling, "would be receptive to after-hours service, so they can spend time shopping with their spouses."

"After hours?" Hainie half-whispered. "No way, José."

"Another flash idea," Harold said. "But this jail business—"

"Ha!" I said, "Just a way to open up the channels. A market survey technique."

The girl tugged on his hand. "Don't they have hair in jail?"

"Unorthodox," he murmured, cutting a look at Hainie. She turned away to pick up a sleep mat.

"I knew he was joking," Hainie said. She looked him straight in the eye.

"Come on, Chloe," Harold said. "I'll talk to this man another time." They made for the doors, and he said without turning back, "Hold off on the market research. Let's take it step by step."

Hainie plopped onto a kid-sized table, folded her legs underneath her, and let her chin down onto her right palm. I sank next to her on the floor. She ran the fingers of her left hand over the back of my head. "You and your bristly head."

"So you'll love me even if my wicked ways take me to jail?" I said.

Her eyes shifted. "Not if, baby. When." She recrossed her legs.

"Don't you have faith in your old man?" I said, smiling.

"I have faith in *us*." I still don't know how she managed to make that sound like a warning.

CORAL, FROM THE SEA

GERRY knocked on the trailer's front door again. She couldn't help glancing at the windows where simple white shades were hanging. The windows would be where a burglar would enter, not the door (if a burglar were hard up enough to break into a trailer). A yellow plastic cat reclined below a trellis to the left.

It didn't make sense rejiggering the locks on a trailer, but you do what a client wants, as long as they can pay. Gerry figured that the money Merlin's clients paid for wasted effort could stretch all the way to Denver. And a lot of that came from folks on the trailer stretch of Route 1, where she was now. The main thing was to turn the money into something better for her boy Marty.

Suddenly she felt a hot blast and the very windows she was eyeing blew out with the force of what the fire marshal later called an "overpressure." Like popping a massive plastic bag. One of the shades sailed out onto the grass, propelled by a knickknack that now lay beside it.

Gerry didn't hear the blast, of course, but she felt a light smack of a pressure wave.

Joe, at the office, would play off her deafness with stupid stunts like talking to her while filing a key, just to see her answer when any hearing person wouldn't have known what he had said at all. It was stupid, but it showed he was proud of her. "My rookie," he called her still, after two years. It was better than the treatment she had gotten from the born-deaf crowd at Gallaudet. That's what she told people.

"They got all these little groups," she'd say. "There's American Sign Language and English, you get put off in one little group. Lip readers get put in another. Everyone's got a pigeonhole. And they *hate* hearing people. I'd say, 'There's a big world of hearing people out there.' It drove them nuts. They couldn't *stand* it."

Gerry had gone deaf at fifteen, it just seemed like one more in a string of accidents that were headed her way, in part because she was stubborn. Soccer, volleyball, field hockey. She went at them as if she were killing snakes, the body be damned.

Moments after the blast, she could tell that someone inside the trailer was yelling. She glimpsed the movement through the window, then an older woman opened the door, still in her nightgown. She was yelling back at someone inside.

"Are you all right, ma'am?" Gerry asked.

The woman had two strands of grey hair falling down on either side of her face, which was flushed. She had hazel eyes and a gap in her lower teeth that kept flashing as she spoke. Gerry had to urge her to slow down so she could understand.

"I'm fine," the woman said, more slowly. "Fine. It's my son who's upset."

A half-dressed man flashed by the doorway behind her.

"What happened?" Gerry said.

"Nothing," the woman said. "I saw a cockroach in the sink. A couple of—" The woman turned away inside and was yelling fast again, so Gerry lost what she said. There was smoke lifting off the tops of the windows.

"I got a call that you wanted to change a lock," Gerry said.

"No point in that now, we got no windows," the woman said. "I'm sorry. I eff-ed up."

Gerry missed the last bit.

The man appeared again, this time in a pea-green Virginia Tech sweatshirt. "I'm sorry about this," he said. "My mother just set off a fist full of bug bombs in the kitchen. I think the stove blew 'em up."

Gerry asked him to say it again, to make sure she got it right. He wasn't bad-looking—his eyes were almost silver, and from his neck and arms he looked like he'd been a high school athlete, back before he'd gained a few pounds and his hair had gone pepper-and-salt.

"Bug bombs," he repeated, slow. "She's nuts." He looked wrung out.

"Sorry to hear it," Gerry said. "About the bugs, I mean." She saw the trailer's front wall had bowed out from the blast. At the bottom it sagged like a stack of slick magazines.

"She sees one bug, they all gotta die," the man said. He stuck out his hand. "My name's Ray."

"Mine's Gerry." She pointed to the name tag on her uniform.

"I can read," he said.

"Sure you're all right?" Gerry said.

The man scratched the back of his neck.

"Well, you folks give a call when you want new locks," she said. She turned to leave.

When she glanced back, the mother was saying something.

Gerry turned to see. "We'll need them locks changed sometime. In case Al comes around."

"Al's my brother," Ray said. "He's a bad egg."

"He's not a bad egg," the mother said. "He's just upset."

"We'll carve it on his headstone: 'He was upset.'"

There was a distant rumble on a low register, like the bleeting of a fire engine.

Gerry hated Route 1. It bred mean, ignorant people. People so ignorant you felt bad for hating them. Joe knew she felt that way. It was cruel of him to send her on trailer park jobs. Lots of Merlin Locks' business came from tonier suburbs around Mount Vernon, where people got the jitters after reports of a burglary. But along the strip of apartments and warren of duplexes off Route 1, break-ins didn't scare folks as much. Joe said it was because people there trusted folks more. Gerry thought of her father, and said bullshit.

"You folks take care," she said to Ray.

"Wait!"

But Gerry kept walking to the van. She sensed a commotion behind her. She turned.

"You forgot something!" He was waving a hand.

"What's that?"

"Your card," he said. "Give me your card."

She fished into her breast pocket for one. A woman seated on a step in front of the house across the narrow access road was talking on a cordless phone. Excitedly, looking at the smoke that was still oozing out of Ray and his mother's trailer.

The fire-engine rumble was getting close, and there was the shudder of a horn blast.

Just for a second, her hand still in her pocket, turning to look past Ray to where the fire engine was coming from, Gerry thought of Marty. She wondered what he was doing, and felt a sudden rush of relief that he would never meet this guy Ray.

She handed Ray a card and headed back to the van. She sat there for a couple of minutes, watching the firemen in their bulky jackets with the yellow reflector stripe talk with Ray's mother. Smoke continued to seep from the windows. The emergency workers looked casual, curious more than anything. Gerry watched as one fire helmet inside moved from window to window. They'd be checking for gas leaks, she guessed. Ray's mother was gesturing to the two firemen and the neighbor with the phone, who had wandered over. She was a histrionic old woman. Gerry watched the spectacle of trailer chatter and fire truck a minute more, then switched on the ignition.

Back in Wilmington when she was growing up, trailers were the site of all the world's craziness and depravity. "Monsters" is what her father called the people who lived there. He'd fold the newspaper and say, "Those monsters off 610 have been at it again." Or, "Had a monster come into the office today, complaining about the hookup. If they paid their bills, they wouldn't have a problem."

Her father would say that with that half-smirk of his, the same one that, after her accident, made it so hard to read his lips. But she could turn off her aid in a fury and, seeing that smirk, know what he was saying. Know that, when she got pregnant, he was comparing her to the monsters. She knew without watching his lips that he was calling Marty a little monster-to-be.

It was cruel for Joe to send her to these places, she thought again as she started up the van. And she'd tell him so when she got back to the Merlin shop.

SHE WASN'T PREPARED when she went to an address three days later, a squared-off, brick-a-brack apartment in Huntington, and Ray's mother came to the door. For a second, Gerry couldn't place her.

"You're the locksmith," the woman said. "I remember. My name's Audrey. We're staying here with my sister until our place is ready. Such a stupid accident."

She explained they wanted the lock on the apartment's front door changed.

Gerry was a little rattled, but she set down her tool box and got to work. It was a standard model Schlage deadbolt, sturdy enough. Audrey just wanted to change the key on it.

Gerry kept her eyes down and her focus on the door. She didn't want to look into the apartment and see Ray. She imagined him in a lounger with his feet up, watching t.v. She didn't want to think about the brother, who was probably motivating this lock change like he had at the trailer park. These were seedy people.

She had the cylinder broken out in two minutes. She hoped she could use the same bolt and strike plate, just swap the cylinder, but it was an older model and it looked like that wasn't going to work. She sighed, realized she'd left the chisel in the van. Just then she realized someone was standing nearby.

The buzz of syllables from her aid sounded like: "How's it going, lady locksmith?"

She looked up just for a second. "Hard to say, Ray. How about you?"

"Can't complain, I guess."

"Lucky you got your aunt here to stay with." She turned from him, back to the door. "Are we doing this because of your brother?" she said.

She didn't want to watch his answer, didn't know why she'd asked. She heard just a low murmur.

"Uh-huh," she said.

After a minute, Ray walked away. Gerry got the shaft for the new bolt drilled out. Then she went back to the van and got the chisel, and scraped the bed for the strike plate clean. She was nearly done in a half hour, and impressed with herself.

"Not bad for a rookie, eh, Joe?" she said as she slipped the cylinder into place.

"Not bad at all." She turned and saw Ray there again.

"I guess your brother won't hassle your mom now," she said. "So what did he do, anyway?" Gerry was feeling powerful, good about herself, so she didn't really contain herself like she should've, she realized.

"Some folks say he robbed them," Ray said with a half-smile. "Main thing is, he called and asked Momma for money. He's a loose wire. When Al asks for money, he doesn't fill out an application." Ray shook his head, rubbed his left hand over the hair of his right forearm. "So were you born deaf?" he asked.

Because she was feeling strong, she told him about the field hockey accident. It seemed to quieten him a bit. So she told him about breaking her wrist playing volleyball, and how the doctor had to set the bone with pins and take part of her hip bone as replacement.

"He said they might have to take more, but I said no. So they used coral. From the sea. Cool, huh?"

"Cool." Ray looked a little remote.

She said, "I got hit in the eye with a softball once, so I'm practically blind in my left eye. And in my work, my eyes are my ears. Makes it hard."

"Huh," said Ray. "You're hard on yourself, aren't you?"

"Nope. Think so?" She twisted the key in the lock, shot the bolt back and forth. "I just like sports. I go all out. I don't hold back."

Ray eyed her without saying anything. He wasn't too bright, she figured.

Joe had his own theory about her injuries, which he repeated over and over. "You can't get used to the fact you're a woman," he'd say. "You keep calling on your body like it's a man's, and when it can't stretch that far, you get hurt."

Joe looked real smug saying that. He couldn't believe she'd really go to Denver.

As Gerry saw it, the problem was that her reflexes were too slow. She'd push herself through batting practice, through spike and defense leaps, through stick practice on the field. Her reactions improved, but her eye was faster than her reflexes. Or had been.

Her father had a theory too. She didn't like to think about it.

"Ma'am?" she called into the apartment, past Ray, who was still standing in the foyer.

"What's that?" Ray's mother came bustling into the hall.

"She's finished, Ma."

"Well look at that. You're so fast! Now Ray, you should have a skill like that. See how fast she did that? Why, I bet she makes good money doing that."

"That'll be fifty dollars," Gerry said with a grin.

"You take a check? I hate to borrow from Doris. And Ray's no good for it." The old woman poked her son.

"Yes, ma'am," Gerry said.

By the time she left, Gerry almost felt sorry for Ray. But she was glad to be gone.

GERRY'S FATHER did a job all right. His story of passing the shacks in the alley on his way to school when he was a boy, the sour smells and sad cries of wartime Wilmington. "Self respect," he said. That's what he learned. "You have to take yourself seriously. Or nobody else will." Not that his mother's apartment was so much nicer for it.

He told the story over and over, it got more frequent when she went to Gallaudet—the deaf college.

Gerry had seen her father uncomfortable only twice, and both times it was on the Gallaudet campus. He came there once to bring her mother for a visit Gerry's first semester, and the second time to help Gerry move her things when she dropped out. Both times he never said a word out of line, but moved with purpose, like he was crossing alien terrain. He parked the station wagon, he flipped down his shades, he got from Point A to Point B. When they reached her new apartment, the second time, and he sank into the old overstuffed blue chair that they'd struggled up three flights of stairs, he breathed like he'd survived a battle. He looked around and said, "I guess this place is as safe as most places you've been." His face was killer.

"Take yourself seriously."

On the field, that's what she did. Complete focus. And that's what she brought to the locks, whether they were smooth new fingerprint pads or old tumbler boxes. They were puzzles she could take seriously, and solve. That's why she sometimes told Marty about them—she wanted to show him a part of her she liked.

Her father eventually warmed to Marty, probably because he saw something of himself in the boy's face, the skinny calves. Nothing more than tribalism. The old man came for the day now and then. When she saw them come in the door together, yakking about Ripken, she felt a bitter love—the grating bond that held them together without giving her the respect he harped about. It was bitter love, and she worried that it could turn poisonous.

She ran into Ray in Jerry's Subs on Route 1 two weeks later, when she was rushing lunch between two jobs that Joe had set up way too close together. She was trying to keep the sauce in her meatball sub from dripping onto her uniform when someone tapped her shoulder.

"Hey," he said, "how's the break-in business?"

She tried to stay cool, but it flustered her. "Keeping me busy," she said, and made a point of laughing. "Pays the bills. How's your mother?"

"Okay. We moved back into the trailer. A *new* trailer," he said. "They hauled the old one away. How's Marty?"

This shook her even harder. She didn't remember mentioning her son to these people. It made her scared, in the grim fluorescence of Jerry's, to see Marty's name on this guy's lips.

"Gotta go. I have another call," she said. "See you around."

When she picked up Marty late that afternoon, she found herself looking around the school entrance for suspicious characters.

"How was school?" she asked.

"Fine," he said. In profile, his snub nose looked exactly like her father's in old photos.

It was generally not a good idea to talk with him while she drove, it wasn't safe. Usually, she sidestepped the problem by unreeling a monologue, about her plans for their move out to Denver, new security technologies she was learning (he perked up when she talked about the fingerprint and eye signature technologies she was reading up on), his fake eyeball collection, or anything else that occurred to her. She knew it was good for kids to have a lot of stimulation, and she thought by sharing all the thoughts that rattled around in her head, she could do that for Marty. Sometimes it came out as worry.

But Marty never objected. He had grown up as man of the house. In that sense, Gerry joked, puberty would be a step backwards.

When they got out of the car, Marty hitched his backpack onto his shoulder and said, "I don't want to go to Denver."

"Sure you do, it's beautiful out there," she said. They started up the stairs to the apartment. "Remember when we went hiking on Skyline Drive? It's like that, only a hundred times better. The air is cleaner, the mountains taller, the sky bluer."

"I don't know anybody out there," he said.

"You'll make new friends." She smiled. "You just don't want to miss Ripken's last game."

"That's not it," he griped. "It's a stupid idea."

"Hey, watch your mouth, young man. It's your mother's idea."

Marty would turn ten in two months, but he was already showing signs of looming adolescence. Fastidious combing of the hair, for one thing. Her sister with three boys said that was the six-month advance warning of puberty. Gerry couldn't believe it. Ten years old!

"*You* don't know anyone in Denver either," he said. "You don't have a job there. What's out there?"

"The good life," she said. "You'll see."

She was putting boxes in the cupboard but she could tell he had said something.

"What was that?" She turned to him.

"Nothing."

She stared him down, level. "You don't do that," she said.

He twitched in his seat a moment. "Sorry," he said.

"I forgive you," she said.

"But I don't want to go."

"Why not?"

"I already said! Why do *you* want to *go*?"

She looked at him, his part straight as a paper cut through the sheaves of dark umber hair, this late in the day. Adolescent. He was catching up to her, and she was still racing away from *her* folks.

"WE GOT A CALL from your friend in the trailer park," Joe said when she came in the next morning. "She asked for you by name."

"What the hell?" She slammed down her box of lock pins on the counter. "You're kidding, right? They just got a brand new trailer, they can't need new locks already!"

He blinked. "How do you know that?"

She said she'd run into Ray at the sub shop the other day. "Christ, Joe, just tell them I didn't come in. Give it to Hermie. If I see those people one more time I'll have to detox." She almost said 'those monsters.' What she said was, "They give me the creeps."

"Gerry," Joe said, "the woman asked for you."

"*Joe*," she said, mimicking his pleading eyes, "screw you!"

She ended up going. The new trailer was in the same spot as the old one. The other trailers herring-boned off from the service road, some with deco-like fins waving up, one with 'Detroiter' labeled onto the roofline in mailbox letters. She passed a parked Chevy, and a shiny green Ford 4x4. The turf around the new blue-trimmed trailer was cut up and muddy from the move. Again, Gerry felt herself tightening inside at the embarrassing intimacy of poverty. The same neighbor was sitting on her front step across the road with her cordless phone to her ear as Gerry knocked on the door. She wondered how anybody here could afford new cars.

The old woman came to the door. "Here you are!" she said. "Our lady of the locks!"

Gerry couldn't help laughing. But a look at the door sobered her up. "How is it we're changing locks on a new door?" she asked, trying to hide her irritation.

"I gave a key to Al," the woman said, shaking her head, "in a weak moment. I thought he was better. I wanted to…" Her voice trailed off.

Gerry couldn't think of what to say. "You don't got any bugs, do you?" she said lamely.

"Nope," Audrey said. "Not a one. You?"

"Just my boy," Gerry said impulsively, "but he's a good one."

"Like my Ray."

Gerry jerked up from the lock she'd begun to inspect. She wanted to spit something out at the woman, that Marty was in no way like Ray. She clenched her jaw, had to suppress herself really hard not to say anything, not to look the woman in the eye. These people were ignorant, that's all there was to it. No need to hate them for it. But she felt like she was grinding her teeth keeping her mouth shut. Mean-spirited ignorance was what it was. And the sooner she got Marty away from here, the better. She wouldn't raise him in a place where he'd get mistaken for this woman's trailer trash. In Denver he'd be judged by the content of his character. Which was A plus plus, by the way.

The door was hollow and the sides were cheap half-inch

plywood, so she was having trouble getting the lock positioned. With all the trailers she'd done, it was the first time this had ever happened to her. It was because the materials she was dealing with were for shit. She would make sure Joe understood that. But maybe she could work it, at least a temporary solution.

She twisted the knob left and right, checking the bolt action, seeing if it would hold. Maybe for a week. Gerry started blinking quickly, like when onions burned her eyes. If she left them closed even for a second she saw her father talking to her.

Then the bolt wouldn't retract. She slapped the door. "Goddammit," she said. She'd have to call Joe.

Suddenly the old woman was there. She asked if anything was wrong.

"Nothing," Gerry said tightly.

"I wasn't born yesterday, honey," Audrey said. "I can see something's—"

"I need something from the truck," Gerry barked. "You know this door won't protect you from bad eggs, no matter what lock we put on it."

She stalked out to the van, climbed into the driver's seat. She rested her arms on the steering wheel while she gained control of her breath. Her forehead went down against the rim, just for a moment. Then she sat up and started to call in to Joe, looking at the radio set's TTY display. It said, "What's up, Gerry?"

"Joe, I need you to come out here and finish this," she said, holding her voice down. "Their door is hollow, their mechanism is crap, and I can't deal. These are your folks now. Sorry," she added, though she didn't feel that way.

She watched the display. "My rookie's bailing on me?" it said finally.

She exhaled and looked around at the trailers. "Just come out here, would ya, Joe? I'll cover the counter." She stared down at the brake and gas pedals for a few moments, then turned to the display.

"Well come back here, then," it said. It stayed like that for ten seconds or so, then went blank.

COUNTERFEIT

As they walked into the village at the edge of the Kathmandu valley. Howard and Alexa felt accordion music coming from every building. Wedding music, the old woman told them. They sat down on red foam cushions on the floor of the front room that served as the lobby. Alexa held her hemp purse on her lap. Howard's elbow rested on the backpack. They looked out the windows, set low in the thick plaster walls. Breathless, rambling accordion melodies outside churned time into a kind of ether. Howard couldn't tell how long they had sat in silence.

"You *like* to get lost," Alexa had said on the path a half hour before. "Like in Hanoi. It's some perverse pleasure for you."

"That's ridiculous," he said.

"You like to test your luck. It's selfish."

The afternoon had turned sour after they'd left Panauti, a village five miles away. A local festival there had made Panauti magical. Women strolled by in bright copper saris and a man hawked sweets from an ancient cart. "I feel like we just stumbled into a movie," Alexa had said, passing the plastic water bottle to Howard. The scene felt joyous. It was the kind of surprise he had wanted to show her for the months since they'd started their world tour. "This is what it really is," he said.

A couple of hours out of Panauti along the edge of the Kathmandu Valley, they seemed to be off their map, a xerox folded in Howard's pocket. It was true, he had tried a shortcut. They approached what looked like a dump, mounds of trash. Howard had stopped and asked a thin woman seated in a doorway, "Which way to Dhulikel?"

The woman had smiled and pointed back along the path they were on. They were so turned around they'd walked right past it. She led them to the lodge. She was the one who explained to them about the wedding music.

Howard was not acting like a safety officer of a nuclear power plant, which was what he was back in Madison. (He was so used to Homer Simpson jokes that he'd fallen into the stupid habit of uttering "Doh!" when surprised.) Here he was taking shortcuts, eating fried dough that looked like it had been on the vendor's cart for days. He and Alexa had been traveling since mid-January, and now, halfway through the trip, he seemed to be reaching some crisis. They had intended this world tour as a last fling before settling down, but now Howard seemed to be having some weird reaction. He wanted to keep traveling forever.

"Nepali people are crazy!" cried a young Nepali man who burst through a curtain of beads at the far end of the lobby.

That was the manager of the lodge. It was an apology. A group of sixty officials from the city had just checked out, and the place was a mess.

"All night, fighting, yelling, glasses broken, police!" The manager rolled his big buckshot eyes. "Very sorry to keep you waiting."

They asked to see a room, and he led them upstairs, a room

just off the staircase. Alexa peered in, her dark shoulder-length hair glinting with light from the window beyond. She asked to see another. After four months on the road, she could suss a room's downsides in seconds.

The manager showed them another room, monastic but airier than the first: two twin beds, old double doors that closed with a large gray wooden dead bolt, a candle niche deep in the plaster wall. A cedar in the courtyard rested a branch on the window ledge.

"Wonderful," Alexa said, looking out the window. "Fine." She sank down onto one of the tack mattresses.

"We'll take it," Howard said. The tautness in his face was relieved by his hair. He'd given up parting it, so it curled wherever it wanted to over his forehead.

"How do you feel?" he said, after the manager had left.

"Okay," she said. Howard knew that tone. It meant don't ask more, I'll be okay. Sometimes he forgot how strange parts of this trip were. It was his blind spot. Their evenings back in Madison, discussing travel plans, seemed ages ago. Talking about Asia then, Alexa had looked excited and a little at sea— rare for her, and very appealing. Howard had been to Nepal once before, and so had taken the lead in making arrangements for this leg of the trip.

"We can push the beds together," Alexa said. She flashed her first smile since the morning. "I'll feel better after a shower." She took a towel and the little shampoo container and went in search of the shower.

Howard walked out to the garden behind the lobby, where three white tables were set. How could they have walked right past this place? He sat and ordered a Sprite for Alexa and a Star beer for himself. As the sun went down, he sipped the beer and skimmed the guide book, looking up from time to time at the shoulder-high wildflowers, white and red.

He read about Lumpini again. The Buddha's birthplace was the one spot in Nepal that excited him. It seemed like it should hold something for them, some surprise or lesson. They could cover the 100 or so miles west from Kathmandu the next day, down from the hills to the terai plateau. After that, they could leave the subcontinent, move on to Africa.

Alexa joined him at the table. The moon rose over the garden, through ragged white holes in clouds to the east.

"Good shower?" Howard said.

Alexa made a face. "Not great. But I do feel better."

"Sorry about the shortcut."

"Let's leave it. What are you reading?"

"Oh, stuff." He didn't want to talk about the bus ride to Lumpini just now. When they'd discussed it before, Alexa had teased him about his enthusiasm. "You think we'll get enlightened?" she'd said.

It got darker and they ordered dinner. The waiter was a boy full of giggles, which came off as insolence. "Which should I pour first, sir?" he said, waving the water pitcher over their glasses.

"Doesn't matter."

"Oh *thank* you, sir," the waiter tittered. Soon he was asking them questions. And what did Howard do for a living?

"Wildlife research," Howard said. He had no intention of fending off more broadsides about nuclear holocausts.

"Animals? Oh yes, *save* the animals!" The boy laughed again. He asked where they were from, what they thought of Nepal, if they had children.

Alexa managed to turn the interrogation around. The boy

answered he had one child, a son. "Here, if the first child is a boy, big party," he said. "If a girl, no party."

He was just twenty-three. His wife was fourteen when they married four years ago, he said. "We are ethnic people, sir," he said apologetically.

The waiter had a good face and a chipped tooth. "I want to have another child, but she doesn't. We are always talking about this. And excuse me, will you be having children?"

"Not tonight," Alexa said. "We're still too young."

The boy nearly whooped. "Oh yes!" he cried.

They ate their chicken butter masala and chips, and watched the lights in the lobby.

Howard started to ask how she was feeling again, then reconsidered. Instead, he talked about the people they'd seen in Panauti. It seemed the start of a genuine phase of their trip, now that they had toughened as travelers together. He looked forward to Lumpini.

THE BUS RIDE the next morning did them in: an achingly hot trip down hairpin curves, much of it on roads washed-out by the last rains. The windows were sealed shut. The AC wasn't working and they were poached in sweat.

"We've got to open these windows," Howard told the bus conductor. "There must be a way." They were packed in three to a seat. The middle-aged German at Howard's elbow said, "This is outrageous." But the conductor explained that the bus was made exclusively for AC comfort. "The windows are sealed."

"My wife isn't feeling well," Howard said. "Can you do something?"

At dusk, the driver stopped at a roadside shanty. Alexa

looked sadly at the hill girls who huddled together giggling. One of the girls paraded a cat on her head for the foreigners.

Well after dark, the driver stopped at a lodge in a no-name town and the passengers filed to the check-in desk. When Howard asked, the driver told him it was at least another day's ride to Lumpini. The road was worse than he'd expected.

Howard felt demolished. In their room, he dropped their bags as Alexa flopped onto the low, soft mattress.

"This sucks," he said. "What do you want to eat?"

"Nothing," she said, her arm crooked over her face. "I can't eat. You go ahead. I can't take another day on that bus. I'll die."

"Please don't," he said.

"This feels really, really bad."

Howard still stood, wondering what that meant for the next day.

"We're crazy," she said.

"What do you mean?"

"We make these crazy decisions on the spur of the moment, with no information, then we're flabbergasted when they don't work out." She moved her hand away from her face and looked upside down at him. "Are we adults?"

"We're *young* adults," he deadpanned. "We're not ethnic people. We're adventurers."

"We're nuts!" She covered her face again.

"I'll bring you something."

He set off past the palms outside their room. The palms were another sign they'd left the mountains. He felt like a palm himself, his head a clutch of coconuts and leaves bobbing high in the wind, no sturdy trunk or roots beneath. Walking along the dirt road's seam of rocks and cans, he felt old and empty, and that he'd shamelessly misled Alexa. He prayed that she was not really sick.

To distract himself he focused on what he saw: melancholy young women on bicycles. A boy's tray of carefully arranged coconut slices—when he spun the tray it blurred white like a crown. A woman in a red velveteen top stopped to talk with an elderly man. A bus passed, with a gaunt male face peering out the broken back window, fingers gripping the jagged glass.

When Howard stalked back through the lodge with a greasy bag of curry, the bus conductor was in the lobby. He smiled and waved to Howard. He can fuck himself, Howard thought, waving back.

By the time Howard reached the room, he had given up his dream of seeing Lumpini. It was too much. He didn't know what they'd do, but they had to change plans.

On the way to the lodge, the bus had passed what looked like a rundown airport tower. If it was an airport, he and Alexa would fly back to Kathmandu and check the hospital there, or fly on to Delhi.

The room swam in dingy yellow light. Alexa was feeling worse, curled up on the edge of the bed. "That woman behind us on the bus is probably dreaming of Shanghai," she said. "That's where her sister is vacationing. She kept saying, 'I could be with my sister now.'"

Howard laughed.

"I wish *I* was in Shanghai," Alexa said.

"I hear bad things about Shanghai."

"I don't *care*."

They talked about options between Delhi and Kathmandu, but there were many unknowns and Howard wasn't thinking clearly. After a long time he agreed to get plane tickets for Kathmandu in the morning.

At breakfast, the plates on the long table were smeared with orange and dark red jellies, and the residue of white toast and egg yolk. Alexa had to race back to the room, but first she pulled two crips 100-dollar bills from her purse and pressed them into Howard's hand for the tickets.

"Will you be all right?" the woman with the sister in Shanghai asked Alexa.

Her concerned tone startled Howard. Had she divined something about Alexa's condition that he didn't know?

Howard walked ten minutes along the road to the airport. It looked worse in the daylight. The runway was just a long grassy field where goats grazed. The airline manager had gone to temple, a check-in clerk informed Howard.

Howard stepped out front to consider how long to wait. Four boys were playing a game on the cement apron there, like craps played with bottle caps and a stone. He watched them for some time.

Eventually the manager walked up, a thin man with a moustache and a reserved bearing, and brown trousers that were too short. His face was deeply lined. Howard explained that he needed two tickets to Kathmandu for that day. The manager tilted his head to the side in a gesture that urged patience.

"Perhaps," he said. "Come back at ten o'clock."

"So?" Alexa said when Howard came back. She was curled up and felt hot.

"There's only one empty seat left on today's flight. But there may be a cancellation."

"Fat chance."

"Who knows?"

"So we buy the last ticket and hope someone cancels?"

Howard said, "I think it's our best bet."

When Howard returned to the airport at 10 (the Germans and the conductor waved goodbye from the bus), there was no change: the manager still said perhaps.

"My wife is sick," Howard said. "Can't you get us both on today?"

"I'm sorry," the manager shook his head. "I cannot know. Please be patient."

Standing on the airport's bare cement floor, Howard saw the tickets as an infuriating algebra problem, or a question of probability that he might encounter at the plant back in Madison. He thought: Should I buy one for today and one for tomorrow, gambling to use both today (*like a man*, he heard a voice say), but allowing at least for Alexa to go alone if there was no cancellation? Or do I cautiously buy two tickets for tomorrow, and risk losing today's remaining free seat?

Beneath this calculation, he sensed another: Do I improve my chances with this guy if I take the risk, or do I set myself up for a fleecing?

Howard asked the manager a few more questions. He sensed an exact subtlety in everything that was spoken and everything left unsaid. He felt he had to divine the options in the pauses in between.

He hedged. He bought one ticket for the next day, Wednesday, and decided to wait until later to buy the second ticket. He handed the manager one of Alexa's hundred-dollar bills, and walked back to the lodge.

By late morning the terai heat was cranking up, and the air over the runway's grass was wavy. On the road five or six boys approached with red bottle-cap goggles strapped over their eyes, with shrill bleating whistles in their mouths. One carried a red balloon. They stopped and stared at him.

"Did the airplane arrive?" he asked them.

One of the boys blew his whistle.

The airport yard was ablur with movement, coils of people laughing, like a Breughel come to life. The deep red powder of tika shone on men's foreheads. A drunk lurched out of the entrance for just a moment before going back in.

The goats had abandoned the runway for the shade under a cluster of large trees. When Howard stepped inside, he saw a dozen passengers with their luggage, waiting for the afternoon flight.

"Ah! You're here." The manager pointed Howard to a dark plastic couch behind the desk, then resumed a discussion with a middle-aged woman in front of the counter. She looked well-off, judging by the gilt in her sari and her large gold earrings.

Howard sat for fifteen minutes, watching as children weighed themselves on the wide metal baggage scale. He wished he knew the right interval after which he should press his case. Patience was valued in Nepal, and he would be a typical Western capitalist if he stormed up and interrupted the man's attempt to hit on a rich woman. On the other hand, Nepalis with high status were rarely patient, so perhaps the manager needed fireworks before acting. The squeaky wheel—

"Excuse me," the manager interrupted. He waved a hundred-dollar bill at Howard. "Do you have another of these?"

Howard nodded guardedly.

"Will you exchange it for this? There's a *very* small tear at the bottom corner here. The bank here won't take it, but in Kathmandu, no problem." Something about the man's smile reminded Howard of the waiter in Dhulikel.

He took the note and inspected it. He laid it on his left knee beside his remaining hundred. Ben Franklin looked up at him with tight-lipped contempt from both knees. They looked the same, but Howard was no treasury expert.

Was this the transparent gambit that it seemed? The eleventh-hour timing, Howard's waiting on the couch, everything suggested that the manager was using leverage to make a counterfeit bargain. But was Howard really losing one hundred dollars, or was he being paranoid in a fist-hearted, American way? He tried to see the question another way: Which would help get Alexa to Kathmandu?

All he knew for sure was that the manager held in his hands their only chance to escape this pit. Howard closed his eyes for a second and he could almost hear Alexa's voice. When he opened them, he traded the bill for the one resting on his right knee.

As soon as he handed over the bill, Howard realized that he had just squandered his leverage for prying another seat out of the manager. He cursed his inexperience with bribery. If only he knew the lingo! Eventually a man trailing a porter and a noseful of cologne checked in as the last passenger. There was still an empty seat, but no room for Howard. He rushed to get Alexa ready, and felt queasy about sending her alone, feeling unwell. At least they knew where to stay in the city.

Walking out into the bright heat, Howard felt used. But he wasn't even sure he had been. He wanted to lie down.

"Howard, what are we doing?" Alexa asked as he bent to pick up her suitcase.

"It's okay," he said irritably. "We're having the time of our life." He looked out the window. The palm trees looked like extravagant hats in the sun.

BOTTLE

BECAUSE I was preoccupied, I didn't notice the pug-faced oaf when he sat down next to me, with his 'Fighting Yahoos' t-shirt spreading out of his wool jacket. The first thing I caught was the odor—as if he and his jacket had just spent three days straight in Seminole's basement bar.

As soon as I got a whiff, I heard: "I said, aren't you from over in Piney Branch? I know you."

"Got the wrong guy," I said.

This happens all the time. Last Wednesday, a woman walks up and says, "Jerry?" When I told her she was mistaken she said, "You remind me so much of my high school friend!" Is that supposed to mean something to me? Shouldn't she just say, "Sorry"? Over a couple of beers Schembler and I figured out that what people recognize is my easy-going nature. "Accommodating," said Schembler, with his look. Which translates into, *You put up with too much bullshit.* But those people have me all wrong.

"Yeah?" said the Fighting Yahoo. "I think I got the right guy," he said. "Have a beer?" He took off his camouflage cap and wiped the heel of his hand against his thinning, varnish-colored hair.

I didn't want a beer. A lot of arguments with Irene were

replaying in my head—accusations, her threats to leave, my rambling counter-arguments, all that. A lot of details to keep on top of. Little things like the drapes closed "the wrong way," the laundry left to mildew—I couldn't keep track of it all and she couldn't forget. I had no idea there were so many things two people could disagree on.

Two hours each way to Mass General—that was another one. Why a hospital halfway across the state? Springfield was just as good. But it had to be Mass General to be close to her parents. Over and over during the train ride, I kept coming back to the sight of Irene in that bed, nursing the baby, crying, "You don't give me any choice! No more bottle."

I can't stand trains. You see only the worst sides of towns from trains—deserted railyards and abandoned warehouses, graffiti like overinflated tires, the parts of cities that have died. There's a reason why on maps, train lines look like scars.

Back when I was a kid I would have stolen to be on the train into Boston; at night I'd hear it chug out of town and know it was carrying away all mystery and life. But on these trips to see Irene in the hospital I feel every little shake of the car in the floor, seat and window, and every weird bend in the tracks. And I can't stand the rank metal toilets or the heat of the sandwich bar. Amtrak ruined trains for me.

This morning it meant another four hours away from work, another chance for Schembler to give me that look when I asked.

"Go ahead," he said, "this job's never gonna get finished," he said, waving his wire cutters at the nest of cable in the bare frame ceiling. "Fuck it." Schembler can say a lot with those bushy eyebrows. But he knew Irene and I had to get this straightened out, because she's been threatening for months that she'll leave when the baby comes. I didn't take her seriously. I just heard it as a starting bell for another round, and part of me would yell, "Fine, go! Before we kill each other." Part of me said, "What are you *saying*? Do you know what you're *saying*?"

The Fighting Yahoo messed with something under the jacket in his lap. I heard a plastic web snap, and out came a can of Bud.

"No thanks." I smiled. In the face of this bullshit, I smiled.

"I guess I said it wrong. Have a beer." When I still didn't grab it, he stuffed it into the space between my leg and the armrest. After he'd opened it. Then he sat back and grinned.

Soon the train would hit the rough section of track at Gardner, and it would be all over me. I'd smell like a brewery walking into the maternity wing. I took a swig just to bring down the level. It was bitter and already flat. It was warm.

"See?" he said, his eyebrows going up. "It's a good morning for it. I bet you got a reason to celebrate. I got one."

"Look, friend," I said. "I'm going to the hospital to see my wife. I don't need her smelling beer on me at this hour. I won't have a thing to celebrate."

"Your wife's in the hospital?" he said. "She have a baby?"

Like he knew. I was telling him why he should leave me alone, but somehow he knew. He caught me off guard.

"Holy Mother!" he yelled. He was getting louder and louder. "You got a reason for this whole *train* to celebrate. Hey everybody—" He got to his feet, waving his beer over me in the process.

I shut him up fast with an elbow to the gut.

It caught him harder than I intended—a soft, squashy gut. He took a minute to catch his breath. "Still got new dad nerves, don't ya," he wheezed.

"Sorry," I said. "I just want to sit here in peace."

"At least have a beer with me. You can at least do that. To make up."

No MORE bottle, she said yesterday. She made it as simple as possible, like she was talking to a child and she wanted to make sure the kid gets it right. Because the kid's messed himself so many times before, and she's had it. Or maybe it's because we've been talking past each other so much that she chucks all subtlety to make this one point. It's so patronizing.

Sitting up like St. Joan in the starched white bedsheets, with that tiny football of pink flesh in the crook of her arm. What could I say? End of conversation.

But I knew it's not about my drinking, really. She knows I'm no alcoholic, any more than she is. But she put her finger on something, something wrong. When she doesn't infuriate me, I give Irene credit—her mind's always moving, testing what you've said, what she's said.

She was sitting up in the hospital bed. A gust of wind came in the huge window, the sky outside flushed with wind and high, fast-moving clouds, with the light and the clouds nine floors above downtown. My heart was in my mouth. The wind was so strong, the sky a big blue well. And her eyes—big, coffee brown and fierce. I saw her eyes and her chapped hands around the yellow cotton blanket, she was yelling over the roar of the wind, "No more bottle."

"You go into town a lot, Ronny?" The Yahoo was still breathing hard. "I used to go all the time. I haven't been in years. Six years."

How much further with this guy? I wondered. Why did he think my name was Ronny? He had scared off the woman across the aisle. She made like she was getting off the train, but later I saw her plaid scarf through the window in the next car up.

"I used to work for the power utility," he said. "Went everywhere downtown for them, painting lines and pipes." He nodded, his lower lip poking out. "They pay all right, the utility. But always white paint. Why? It's a stupid color."

"Look, sorry but I'm not up for chit-chat this morning," I said, immediately regretting the apology. "And I don't want any more of your beer." There were three empties lined up beside my leg under the metal window frame.

"Sure, fine," he said. "I only got one left anyway. Your timing's perfect."

He got this kicked-dog look. Maybe he thought his face was blank, but it wasn't.

"I told you I didn't want any," I said.

"You were just being polite. I didn't care. I *don't* care. Look!" he said all of a sudden, leaning across me. "See that church there? I was christened in that church."

We were trundling through Leominster. With a stubby forefinger he was wiping at the condensation, smudging the glass where a square little dirty building flashed a second before. I got slammed by a double blast of his jacket and his breath—old burgers, beer, sweat and wool. Between that and the train's motion, the warm flat Bud and the sun's heat burning me through the glass, I rose on a swell of nausea and slumped back.

"Say, you all right, Ronny?"

"I'm feeling a little sick."

"You're white as a sheet."

"Don't worry about me."

"Have another sip. The other day I wasn't feelin' so hot myself. I near fainted, just walking along the highway. I was lucky I didn't fall, I could'a been hit. By a car."

"Lucky," I said.

"You bet. So are you." He waved his can toward me.

The edges of my vision were flickering in and out.

YESTERDAY when I left the hospital I wandered out on the Fenway. It was way the hell in the wrong direction from the station and I was going to be even later than I'd told Schembler, but I didn't care. I felt heavy like I was going to burst and my head and heart and everything was going to pour out on the Fenway's dead brown grass. And the two teenagers sitting over on the wall would just bust out laughing.

My friends laughed, giddy and drunk, last November. Marriage—my marrying—was so funny that night I wiped my eyes laughing so hard. And the next day during the ceremony, I still had the same smile on my face. P.J. and Schembler and everyone told me I looked happy. Irene looked glorious, she truly did. But my cummerbund kept riding up my shirtfront, and I felt the deejay's schmaltz lapping over me. Looking down on myself from the rafters of the auditorium, brown-paper turkey decorations still on the wall. Watching me, I realized how stiff and disconnected I looked compared to Irene, our friends, even my father.

"He's not playing anything on our list," she fumed. She was

just starting to show. And my heart was going crazy. I felt so old so fast.

On the Fenway after I left the hospital, I hardly felt my feet under me, the world was foggy with the deejay's tape of 'YMCA', and Schembler's voice fussing at the tux shop where we got fitted, where I stared up at this wall of cummerbunds. It was a shrine to something horrible. Black-and-white checked ones and lime green and pink and every ugly, tasteless possibility you could imagine. Jesus. Schembler was pointing up at the lime green one and laughing. Those plastic shoes carving into my ankles.

Six years ago I would walk out on the Fenway in the same numb-cold spring weather, same fast-moving sky that scared the shit out of me yesterday, but back then I loved it. Back then the sky made me feel boundless, a little buzzed. Yesterday I wanted to be nineteen and hungry again, desperate for a woman to wrap my big black coat around. Here I *had* a woman —a wife and baby, even—but I wanted *not* to have one, and just to *want* one! Crazy. Back then I had no idea of love. These days the details of it wake me up in cold sweats.

"WHAT A FRIEND we have in Waa-*aayne!*" You wouldn't call it singing except for the way the Yahoo jammed his chin down into his neck to croon the last syllable. "What a friend we have in him!"

Someone up front giggled. A woman turned around and tilted her head. I could see creases at the edges of her mouth. The dingy yellow walls and windows seemed to bristle with eyes.

"Keep it down," I said.

Why didn't I move? It was like sitting next to runny fried

eggs. "What's the matter?" cried Wayne. "I'm their friend. Everybody's friend. They got nothin' to fear from *me*."

It was near the top of his lungs.

The conductor came through the door on the last phrase. "What's the problem?" he said, chin out, strolling toward us in his blue suit and sealegs. The sunlight pegged him at the knees and strung a line of little flags behind him along the aisle; it swung into the seats as the train swerved alongside a grey patch of spiny-branched woods.

"No problem, officer," Wayne said. "Just happy to be here with these good people. Would *you* like something?" He was grappling with the seat in front to haul himself up, one hand pressing down on his armrest. "I was going to get this young man another beer. He can really put them down."

The conductor frowned at me. "It's early for that," he said.

"You're right, sir," I said. "Wayne, I'll pass."

"The hell you say!" barked Wayne. "Officer, my friend here just became a father!"

The conductor smirked, still wary. But the effort made him look less used up. "Congratulations," he said.

The woman up front turned again and I felt more eyes burning into my forehead.

"But you heard him," the conductor told Wayne, "he doesn't want it."

"He's polite. That's why I want to give him a beer. But," Wayne added, splaying his palms out just as the conductor was shifting to make his point again, "it will wait."

"Till you get to the next car," Wayne croaked under his breath once the man had continued down the aisle. He gave me a brat's leer.

"What'd you name it?" said Wayne.

"We haven't yet," I said.

"Haven't named it yet? A little thing without a name?"

"It's only been two days," I said.

"Two days is a long *time* to go without a name," he says, stretching each word to impress on me the sadness of it. "I was doing finishing work on houses in Sioux Falls— don't look at me like that. Sure I do finishing work."

"I didn't say anything."

"Yeah, well, that trip I forgot my name for two days. I was hitching to Omaha, I heard there was work there. I woke up on the shoulder and I couldn't remember my name. Man, was I scared!"

"I bet."

"There was no one to ask. I was afraid if I got a ride they'd ask me my name, and when I couldn't say they'd put me in a hospital. Mother of God, I was scared, but I kept my thumb out. And you know? It came back to me. It turned out all right! Here, have another."

I really wanted to shove this idiot down the aisle with his beer and his stench and his vomit of self-indulgent stories. But suddenly, unwanted, a picture careened into my head of a baby Wayne stretched out on a bay of hospital linen, dreaming feverishly of red and birth-trauma like a case of tremens.

"I'm telling you, you're gonna get me fried," I said. "My wife'll leave me."

He blinked. I could see from his face he was wrestling between taking the beer back to avoid the guilt and his fear of being unfriendly. He didn't do anything.

Looking straight at him, I took a swig from the can. "Where you live now, Wayne?"

"Huh?"

"You didn't tell me where you're living."

"I'm coming back from Ohio." He laughed, suddenly perked up. "Back to Lincoln, Mass. Not long now." He glanced out the window like a prim little grandmother, his elbows pinned back against the armrests. He didn't look at me anymore when he talked.

"Yeah?" I was seeing Irene's face after I kissed her, when she would be taking the smell on my breath as an answer to her ultimatum. I was thinking, 'Certs, drugstore near the station,' but she knows the same as I do what Certs on me at 10 a.m. means. It means bottle. "You got people in Lincoln?"

"Mom and two brothers," he said, nodding hard. "They're meeting me."

"So *you* got something to celebrate, don't you, Wayne?"

He looked at me. He had forgotten his homily earlier, maybe even that he had talked to me before.

"How long you been away?"

"Six years," he said. "Ohio ain't for shit, you know that, Ronny?"

His face was turning gray, a reflection of the high flat clouds that took out the sun. My window cooled off and my head felt better.

"Ohio that bad?" I shouldn't have pried, but I wanted revenge on this guy's warm beer. I wanted some justice.

"Not for *shit*," he said. "Got nothin' for a guy out there."

"Well you picked a helluva time to come back here. There's not shit for you here either, Wayne. Especially in finishing. I got friends in finishing. I've been patching together electrical work for three years. I mean scraping." I shook my head and looked at him sideways. He looked scared.

"Yeah, well hell. Ohio ain't for shit."

A BABY. Unbelievable. Just last Wednesday Irene and I were going at it like two kids. She was after me because I hadn't come straight home from work, so we had missed dinner with her sister. Looking at her, her hair straightened by the pregnancy, it was like looking at a stranger. She was lurching around the apartment, leaning on furniture and shouting, but even the silly pastel maternity dress was like a little girl's. I yelled, "Stop *scolding* me like a *two-year-old*!"

"Stop acting like one," she said.

"Jesus Christ."

"Watch your mouth."

WAYNE thumped his chest. "You don't know, Mike, you got a wife and a baby. You don't know *my* pain. You don't know. You're on the outside."

What a wallowing little asshole this guy was! Pinning me against the window with his crooning self-pity and his miserable brew.

"Thank God," I snorted, and he took a swing at me. His breath caught me first, followed by his thick knuckles on the side of my mouth. Just as I was turning into him, back comes the conductor up the aisle. He lumbered up, his mouth puffing an 'O', and hauls Wayne up and sets him down two rows on, across the aisle. He yelled, "Break it up, will ya," and repeated it like we were a couple of bums.

Everyone was turned around now—the lady with the harsh mouth, the two girls sitting in front of us, Mister Pinstripe across the aisle. Someone behind was staring, I could feel it in the back of my head and neck.

I hadn't had a bloody lip in ten, twelve years. The feeling

doesn't change, though. Same warm, slick tastelessness when you lick it. Same burning in the face. You feel suddenly aware of your teeth, where they are.

When I was ten years old, I got into a fight with my best friend at the bus stop. He had been braying a stupid singsong about me and a girl down the street. I've never been so angry. When he didn't stop, I jumped him. We fought clumsily. The grass was white with frost and I saw the cold steam puffs of his breath, felt my ears aching and numb with the cold and the blows. I sucked on my warm bleeding lip and screamed, my voice breaking with what I thought was victory, "Maybe now you'll keep your big trap shut!"

After the conductor left I glanced down the aisle. Wayne was slowly buckling and unbuckling his belt. Repeating those motions, his thick, round hand—the one I could see— looked like a child's.

I WATCHED myself walk into the hospital with the tendons in the back of my neck tight and dry, like after a drunk, and with all the white and the ethyl alcohol silence of the nurses' rubber-soled shoes—it's like being an astronaut on a new planet. My body was already tightening for another argument, even as I'm picking out a handful of yellow daisies in the gift shop. I would come out and go up to the fifth floor and sink down into one of those molded plastic chairs in the hallway. I could deal with Irene's parents, but her sister better not be there.

Clutching the bouquet, thinking, "Fuck. I'm here to see my wife and my son, and it's eating me up. This is the wrong life." But I would sit and breathe and feel the tightness in my skull and think if I notice it hard enough, it will go away.

FOR FIVE MINUTES Wayne struggled not to speak. Fidgeting, crossing his legs, his eyes skulking his head around. Finally he came back and sat down in the seat next to me again, swinging his head. "You shouldn't have done it," he said.

"Shouldn't have done *what*?" I said.

"You shouldn't have teased me."

"I didn't tease you, you idiot."

"Yes you did. You laughed at me. Anyway, it won't be long now," said Wayne. He looked out the window.

"You ever have a woman, Wayne?" I said.

"Don't start."

"I'm not starting on you. I'm just asking, You ever have a woman? Because they can change you. Yessir. One way or another."

The tracks were rough again. We were rocking side to side and the five Buds were sloshing from ear to ear. He stared down at his belt, buckling it and unbuckling it again like it was a skill he would need soon, maybe at the next stop.

I looked straight ahead to avoid feeling sick, and he mumbled something.

"What's that?" I said.

"I said, 'I know about 'em.'"

"Yeah? Well it's not always bad."

He laughed. "I had a girl in Ohio," he said.

"Yeah?"

"Want to see her picture?"

I shrugged. I should've let him be.

He was tugging the wallet out of his back pocket, it was a struggle. When he got it out I saw it was so old, about to fall apart. The plastic holders for photos and credit cards had turned rust-colored and brittle. I could barely make out the face of the woman looking at me through the yellow web of cracks, but she might have been pretty.

"Her name's Julie. We were steady the whole time I was out there," he said. "Then she left me."

"That's hard. Did she say why?" Did I care?

He was taking a big breath. Suddenly he started bellowing again.

"It's hard, And it's hard, Ain't it hard? To love one that never did love you." It sounded almost like the Guthrie song, but he was lurching across too many keys, full force.

"It's hard, and it's hard, ain't it hard, praise God, to love one that never will be true!"

The train was slowing, I saw a sign saying 'Lincoln' flick by on the platform, and Wayne was singing to the window on the other side of the train, eyes skittering down the tracks. His knees kept bouncing together, then apart. The train stopped with a hiss and one guy at the end of the car stood up and started fooling with a suitcase. Wayne leaned forward, craned around, but didn't leave his seat. Just sat there.

"Lincoln," I said. "You're gonna miss your stop."

"Yeah," he said, clearing his throat, "well." The horn blew.

We were about to move again, when there was some movement on the platform. A door opened at the forward end of our car.

Wayne stood up all of a sudden. "Hey Ronny, you take care of yourself and your little baby," he said. "And don't forget your friend Wayne." He reached up for an olive drab duffle, when two dark state uniforms came down the aisle.

HEADING INTO the hospital, I wasn't thinking about the hand-
cuffs. Wayne was a dull knife next to my own problems. But in
my mind I did see him walking down the aisle, his wrists
crossed in front of him. From behind, he seemed to be just an
overweight slackass shuffling down the aisle to get to the toilet.
Jeans low on his hips. He was squinting out the window, probably checking to see if his mother was on the platform.

I tried to focus: Certs, daisies. In the hallway before her
door I ran my tongue along my lower teeth, paused at the
canine to see if it was loose. I swallowed and blew into my
cupped palms, searching out any unwanted smell.

As my tongue bobbed out to probe the cut on my lip one
last time (I wondered, What will she make of that? What will we
say?)—my stomach balling up on itself already—I realized: My
life has twisted on itself. Some joker like Wayne has given me
the wrong name and a bad set of habits. This baby's dropped in
on the wrong me, and in ten years or so he'll look right through
it all. I felt the dread of that life-sized regret like a wave about
to break on me.

Through the doorway I saw the window, that wide windy
emptiness. I saw Irene sitting up in bed.

I stepped into the room, and began to say something.

ELECTROLYSIS

"Pain levels vary from individual to individual, but pain does not accurately describe the sensation. Electrolysis is much gentler than it first appears."

– West Side Hair Removal Clinic brochure

WHEN he walked through the old lobby with its sign that said, "Visitors Sign In at the Desk," Gary sped up a little. He knew the security guys didn't care, but still he quickened his step, avoided eye contact. This was only his third visit, but already he had become a regular. One guard in particular nodded his big head in Gary's direction every time, but still he avoided the man's gaze.

The guard knew. He was obviously having an affair.

But who would suspect the electrolysis chick on the fifth floor? How would Gary have met her? He didn't see how anyone could piece that together. He was a hairy guy, sure. On meeting Gary, you noticed the bushy eyebrows and the wire brush on the meaty edge of his hand, in line with his little finger, as soon as you shook his paw and he tried to hold you in the grip of his direct-business, beige-eyed gaze. But you wouldn't necessarily see the hairs sprouting from the ridge along the earlobes, or the several on the tip of his nose. And he didn't seem concerned by the hair, or what that meant about how he was aging, or about his appearance at all. You'd think he was all business.

But she put him off guard. On his previous visit, she said she had lived for a while in Arizona, not Phoenix but Flagstaff. It was a place he'd never imagined going.

"Weird atmosphere out there," she said. Denise had a platinum bob and a lovely neck. "You've got half the people former hippies, burn-outs, New Agers. Most of them starting cults of some kind, I'm sure. Then the other half are really right-wing. Young but conservative. It's a weird place." She shivered.

Maybe because she was just wearing panties. Two tattoos stood out on her pale skin: a flower blossom at the small of her back, and a cross near her navel. Both nipples were pierced with gold hoops. Little drawer handles, he thought.

He asked her to push the treatment room door closed. She laughed and walked to where he lay on the bench—a doctor's bench, but covered in a pastel sheet. Near his head was a little electronics set, it looked like the Heathkit project that his father foisted on him when he was a boy.

"Go on," she teased him. "You know you like to give a show." He sighed. She approached the bench and picked up a small wand attachment that rested on the electronics kit.

At this point, Gary found himself again paralyzed with the competing reactions of fear and appreciation of beauty. He hooked his thumbs under the thong on her hips and slid the panties down her thighs. Beautiful skin, white lobes of her buttocks, pearly at their contours.

One thing led to another.

When she was settled on top of him, she held the electrolysis wand so the tip didn't waver from the tuft of hair on his right earlobe. "Don't move," she said with a smile.

Outside the window, through the scrim shade, he could see the yellow top of a schoolbus across the street. His earlobe started to feel very hot.

"What were you doing in Flagstaff?" he asked.

"Going to school. Same as what I'm doing here. At Catholic."

She seemed to be looking at the wall just above the window. He wondered if she could see the schoolbus.

"What are you studying?"

"There, or here?" she said.

He paused, his fingertips behind her left knee. He tried to ignore the flame on his ear, the unbearable delight of her thigh. "Let's start with Flagstaff."

She gave a low giggle. "You sound like my therapist. 'Let's start at the beginning.'" She said it in a low, pompous and syrupy voice.

"In Flagstaff," he said, "what did you study?"

"Mineralogy. Mining. Don't *move*. How to get money out of the ground."

"And what," he said, mimicking her therapist hauteur, "led you to abandon that course?"

"Well, doctor, I was banished for having an affair with my professor," she said. "He got caught and to save his butt he went around telling everyone that I tried to sleep with him for a better grade."

He watched her profile as she said this. She looked bored, as if disappointed with this line of questioning instead of another, like her interest in mining. She had a blemish, maybe it was a mosquito bite, on her cheek.

"Did you?" he said.

She sighed. "I suppose so. So I came to DC."

"And has this been better?"

She nodded. "How's it feel?"

"It feels hot." He wasn't sure if she was talking about the earlobe. It distracted him from mining, and he was finished far too quickly.

THE NEXT TIME he planned *not* to have sex. He had thought about it all morning, all the way to the office. Definitely no sex this time. Just conversation, just the treatment—he was committed to that now, she said it took at least three to eight times, because every hair follicle had at least three hairs. He was practically fibrillating by the time they were in her treatment room. But he was determined not to. He'd turn this thing back to just removing the hair curling off his ears. His erection made it tricky to take off his jockeys.

He was through in two minutes.

They didn't discuss it. Afterward she said, "So, any questions about my studies?"

"None," he said.

She pouted. "I did really well on my geology exam," she offered.

"Great."

"Don't you want to know?"

"Not really." He was getting the hang of this edgy thing, he thought. It created a kind of connection that, in his mid-forties, he wasn't used to.

"You see that café across the street?" She nodded toward the window. "The guy who owns it posted a million five last year."

He looked at the café. It wasn't a franchise. "How do you know that?" he said.

She shrugged. "The point is, there's a lot of it out there," she said. "You've just got to dig it out."

"How about in here?" He waved around at the electrolysis set. "You do all right here, don't you?"

She followed his gesture with her eyes, dully.

THEY HAD first met at a paper convention in the downtown hotel where she gave hair removal demos two afternoons a week. It was a late lunch, and he didn't know anyone at the convention and was suffering a rare episode of self-consciousness, when she appeared at the same table with a tuna wrap from the buffet table. She was younger than most company reps, and he was so charmed and pleased to talk with an attractive woman outside the industry, and she made electrolysis sound so interesting, that he got a little silly.

"Does anyone ever find electrolysis to be a turn-on?" he said.

"Getting their hair fried off?"

"Well—"

"Nobody's ever *told* me they have," she said. Denise had a sweet, goofy smile and that skin, translucent just in front of her ear. She was young enough to be his daughter, but Helen didn't have this much confidence.

"You ever handle See-four?" she said.

It knocked him off balance. It wasn't exactly sexy, but the question lit her face from within like a warm lampshade. In that moment he remembered Marie, the high school crush he sat beside in physics class.

He folded his arms, a gesture that covered his wedding ring.

Much later, someone could ask, What were you thinking? And he'd say, "Nothing. It was nice not to think." He was just curious about C4. He pictured his physics teacher, a mousy older man named Mr. Hinckley, asking the class, "Who here has handled nitroglicerine?" Gary glanced to Marie and arched his eyebrows.

The next thing he knew, he'd made an appointment.

When he showed up at her building on the day, he got cold feet. The old office building made him feel strange and rather antique talking with this young woman behind an office window that had "Hairs off!" painted in swooping white script.

"Fantastic," she said, and motioned him toward a metal chair near the bench. "I'm glad you came. You won't regret this."

"I don't even know what it means."

"Basically, it removes hair with heat. You coagulate the hair follicle," she explained. "Sort of the way jello is made?"

"Terrific," he said. "I'll think of that every time I have parfait. Which is never. So it hurts?"

"No, it doesn't hurt. It tingles."

"I don't want to tingle. I want to talk. How's school? Where are your parents? What do they think of your move to the East Coast?"

"Questions, questions," she sighed. She stepped toward the machine and turned it on. "You'll listen better without all that hair in your ears. You'll look sexier too." She arched her eyebrow.

"Really? You get many men coming for electrolysis?"

She gently pushed him back on the bench. "Just be quiet while I do this. Hold still."

There was the low thrum of a motor and a smell like at the dentist's office or a hairstylist's shop, the smell of something burning.

After fifteen minutes, the pain in his ear had gone beyond the dull hot iron feeling, to numbness. He stopped squirming.

"Maybe that's enough for a first treatment," she said. She took away the wand and turned off the set.

"That didn't hurt so much," he said. "I give excellent back rubs, by the way." He wasn't sure why he said this, it came from a mixture of reciprocity and lust. Mainly the latter. Curiosity too. He hadn't left time for curiosity in his life, it seemed.

She furrowed her brow for a moment in a way that said, *Random!* but then she smiled. "That's sweet," she said. That first time, it was just a back rub.

"So how *did* you get interested in mining?" he asked on his third visit, after the treatment.

"It was a summer job I had with the feds," she said. "A defense contractor."

His eyebrows went up.

"Nothing to do with mines. But I got to blow stuff up."

"You were shooting down nuclear warheads, or what?"

"It was testing, if you *must* know. Checking for tunnels under the DMZ. Korea." She glanced at him, unsure whether he'd heard of the place. "They were digging all these tunnels under the neutral space between north and south. Subversive shit."

"I heard something about it," he said.

"It's supposed to be confidential. So we were checking out equipment for detecting their tunnels. The North Koreans. Which meant I got to set off charges underground to see if the sensors picked it up."

"Cool."

"It was in-*cred*-ibly cool." Her face opened in a smile he hadn't seen since the day he met her. "It was just this little handful of plastic, like Play-doh. Did you have Play-doh as a kid?"

He shook his head. "We just beat rocks together."

"Ha. Well they call it C4. My boss said he used it in Vietnam to heat up cans of spam and shit." She rolled her eyes. "Anyway I had to press this plastic C4 around the detonator, set it in the ground, then walk back along the wire to this bunker. And in the bunker was the detonator."

"I see."

"Not like those big t-bar handles that they push down in the cartoons. It was a bar, but small, and you twisted it." She made a motion with her hands like unscrewing the cap from a pickle jar. "And boom!"

"Wow."

"*So* cool. You feel like hot shit. Powerful, you know?"

"That's what got you into mining?"

She paused. He was massaging her ass, her muscles were taut knots. As he pushed into them, he nearly sent her skidding up the cushion.

"That," she said, "and the fact that you could get that feeling almost every time you went underground. The *earth* thing swept me up." She glanced over her shoulder at him. "Plus the whole mineral wealth thing. Don't forget my neck."

"So, I'm not sure where this is heading," he said, his head cocked to the side to look her in the eye. "We have nothing in common, you know."

"I guess you're right," she said, reaching back and finding his erection. Her fingertips moved along its length. He looked down as if he had never seen it before. He couldn't say anything. Because there was no blood left in his brain. His ear was still on fire, but was that wand doing anything at all?

THE FIFTH TIME he saw her was a stormy afternoon. The sex hadn't gotten any better since that first embarrassment, but they ended each session with a game effort. As he shook the rain out of his umbrella in the lobby now, he was struck by the fact that he kept seeing her *in spite* of the sex. (When he replayed that thought, it didn't quite ring true.) It was the talk, not intimate so much as odd; conversations he had with no one else. About her pet hedgehog (which she got because they required almost no attention), about his days as a ping pong contender (short-lived, long ago). It wasn't really such a shameful affair if the sex was lousy, right? If they kept seeing each other for the talk, he imagined that was less sordid somehow. Perhaps even bohemian. He thought of Henry Miller. This was an exploration.

The elevator opened on the fourth floor and a woman in her sixties stepped inside. "I got off on the wrong floor," she said in a gravelly voice. "So silly."

He gave a thin-lipped smile to validate her embarrassment. Her hair, the firm set of her shoulders reminded him of his wife's Aunt Kate. When they both started off at the fifth floor, he let her go first. She walked down the hall toward Hairs Off!, and he slowed his step behind her. The men's room was in the other direction. He decided to turn back for that stop before seeing whether this Miss Kitty (as he called her in his head) had a de-hairing appointment.

He washed his hands and looked at his image in the purplish fluorescence. He needed to change back, he knew. He was living dangerously and foolishly, and he was having trouble stopping. He never thought beyond the next time. It was a recklessness that he had thought life had ironed out of him. That's what he loved about it. *And yet if I died right this moment*, he thought, *I'd be miserable.* He was struck by how stupid that sounded, and he pushed out into the hallway.

Elsewhere in his life, he had told the mirror in the men's room, he had fulfillments. He did love his wife, and got satisfaction from things as simple as meeting her after work for drinks in Georgetown. Yet for a long time, nothing had been as addictive as this young woman's presence. The parries, the electricity (yes) of watching her eyes dart as she searched for a retort. "Midlife crisis" didn't seem the right word at all. Blossoming. Breakdown. Something like that.

THROUGH the window front of her electrolysis shop, Denise saw him approach down the hall. It was out of the corner of her eye, she was more or less focused on the older woman's chin and its thready hairs, but the movement in the hallway made her glance up and see him. And she realized she had things she wanted to tell him. She threw him a look that said, "This will take a while," and shrugged. He gave a jerky nod, waved, and stepped back into the elevator.

"What is it?" the woman said.

"Nothing," Denise said. "Just someone in the hall."

"It wasn't that man, was it? He was following me earlier."

Denise looked out the back window. "No. This was a woman," she lied.

"It was so strange," the woman said. She had a roundish face and reminded Denise vaguely of Madeline Albright. "I saw him first in the elevator, where he looked nice enough. But when we both got off on this floor I saw this cloud come over his face. I thought he was going to do me in! He started to follow me in the hall, and I got scared. Just for a moment. Then suddenly he wasn't there."

Denise could picture that. She imagined that he could seem a dangerous person. The idea pleased her and made her hope that he came back soon. But the fact was, the thought of him gave her more orgasms than he did in person. Still, you can't have too much of that.

"You can't be too careful," the woman said. "And this floor feels so empty. Those unleased offices. They should replace those lights that are out. Aren't you ever scared?"

Denise smiled. "Have you ever used plastic explosive?" she asked.

HE DIDN'T reappear until late the next day. She was about to lock up. "You didn't call," she said, and immediately wished she hadn't. "Not that I would've picked up. But it can be nice to see that message light blinking happily."

"Maybe that's something we should explore," he said in his therapist's hollow baritone.

"Maybe not." She laughed. Then there came something that hadn't happened since they met in the Marriott dining room: an awkward moment. Separated by the black leather treatment bench, they both stood half-frozen.

"You know," he said, clearing his throat, "Catholic doesn't have a mineralogy program."

"Well, well," she said. "Checking out academics after all those years at the grindstone. Look under engineering. Geotechnical."

He glanced at the certificate on the wall, from the Ft. Collins Institute of Electrolysis. The script looped elegantly through the two 'l's of her last name. Despite the cheap paper, at that moment it seemed to carry more authority than his whole life.

"I believe you," he said. His face flushed and he added, "I feel strange though. Doing this. I've decided I shouldn't come here again."

"Your wife found out?" she said. "Did she ask why you looked so good? And you said—"

"No. She doesn't know. It's just—" He stopped, as if he hadn't thought this conversation all the way through, or had forgotten it.

Denise wasn't going to finish his thought for him. But then she blurted out, "It's just that you lost the *cojones*, right? I'm sorry. I didn't mean to say that."

He continued to cast about the room with his eyes. "I feel like we've been making a bad habit. For both of us."

"Wouldn't want to do *that*," she said. Her voice was firm now. "Sure you don't want another treatment, though? There's still hair coming out your ears."

"Thanks." He smiled stupidly. "I don't think we'd have much to talk about. Then I'd just be smelling my ear burning."

"That's what I'll miss too. The talk. But you won't regret it."

She was wrong, about the electrolysis. He *would* regret it. A few days after, his wife noticed his naked ear, pink and clean like it had never been. She asked what had happened. Startled, he gave a series of inept lies: first he said nothing, then he said his doctor had clipped the hairs to prevent infection, and he followed it up with something ridiculous about laser surgery. When she laughed, he made a show of indignation and complained she was the only one who ever laughed at him. That's when she suspected. She bored right through to the painful truth. He spent a month on a friend's couch, sifting through, convinced his marriage was over. And though they got back together, it would never again be the same.

The episode showed him that this was his life, after all – life with his wife was what he had started, what he wanted. But it made him feel lonely too. (This was a surprise; he was not someone who thought of himself as lonely.) Then he would tug on his earlobe for no good reason.

SPECIAL ECONOMIC ZONE: SHANTOU

THE mini-truck driver laughed as he swerved around the horse cart, brushing the side of the alley. All traffic on that two-lane stretch along the Guangdong coast was headed for Shantou. Knowing that made any danger too ridiculous to care about.

Chang giggled in the passenger seat. "This place is for smuggling," he said into the rearview mirror at Mei, the translator. He gestured to the windshield in a way that took in the whole landscape. The comment was meant for me.

Chang was visibly relieved since he had dispatched his cargo—one of those pint-sized shipping containers that look like a hotel minibar. Tonight he'd be home with his wife. No worries. Mei and I were along for the ride, and soon he wouldn't have to bother with us either.

"Home again, eh, Chang?" I said. He gave a tight smile.

"My grandfather grew up here," Mei said, looking out the window. "He's the one who took the family to Shanghai." She smirked, her head canted against the window. "He never went back."

Chang and Mei were yin and yang. He was fussy about the

rules to success. Mei was a butch hitchhiker from Shanghai who dropped into travel journalism by the simple fact of being an outsider to conventional Chinese life. Apart from Chang's smuggling comment (which didn't count since it was for my benefit), they said nothing to each other the whole ride.

Chang told the driver to stop in the half circle of pavement before the shiny Shantou International Hotel. This was my stop, but I asked Chang to wait and take Mei to the airport. He hedged. It was not convenient.

After an uncomfortable and brief goodbye, he was off.

Even at a big cosmopolitan hotel in this city, I could scatter the front desk staff just by approaching the counter. Only one stood her ground to answer my question: I could find the Internet service on the second floor. It reminded me that Mei was remarkably unflappable in dealing with foreigners and their strange tongues.

After a week in small towns on the coast I felt grungy but I didn't want to delay Mei, so I walked with her to the Bank of China, past rows of vendors selling cheap t-shirts, CDs, DVDs and VCDs. We stopped in a noodle shop; we hadn't eaten all day. Ordered a bowl of porridge and a plate of noodles and veggies. After the claustrophobic air of a smuggling port and Chang's oppressive minivan, Shantou's streets felt refreshingly informal and anonymous. Mei said little but moved more casually than she had in the towns down the coast.

At the bank I followed an elaborate process of chops and ladders, moving from one teller window to the next, showing my passport at no fewer than three stations. Each had to smack the form with their chop, the stamp of Chinese bureaucracy. Mei sat in a plush leather chair looking bored, a misplaced waif in her wool plaid jacket and close-cropped hair. Eventually I counted off six hundred-dollar bills into her hand, one after another. She wrote a receipt, smiled, and we said goodbye.

This is how travel becomes a series of transactions, punctuated with a few vivid images and the flotsam of regret, excitement and recognition.

THE NEXT MORNING I rose up in the elevator to the hotel's twenty-third floor and walked into the revolving restaurant. It had windows on all sides of the circle. Three hundred sixty degrees. The morning sun came off the Yellow Sea in bright pixels and landed against the sides of the other high-rises. Everyone in the restaurant slowly turned toward the park. It felt like a cinematic cliché, like being inside a *Lost in Translation* montage. Easy to have it look multi-layered. Even with no story, the scene contained a piecrust of irony. *This is the world*, it said, *turning in your palm. Your modern world. Ha.*

I ate pancakes in silence, returned to the buffet table for more coffee and a slice of bacon.

Shantou was revolving around me, the skyline new and exploding with energy. Suddenly I felt a powerful contrast with old America, paralyzed by its foggy fear of terrorists. I didn't want to go home. This place felt abundant with opportunity, with hope.

I could make a living here in China, I thought. Doing what? I pushed the pancake slice around my plate. Already three people had mistaken me for an import-export rep. I should take the hint. Refashion myself like Shantou had.

THAT MORNING I walked to the old quarter to see what remained of the foreign trading houses and hotels from China's past. I imagined moving here, renting a room in one of the old places.

There wasn't much left. Block after block of new cement-block shops, then I came to a traffic circle marked by intense remodeling. Cars careened around the circle and spun off onto five arteries. My guidebook said this circle was the last spot where you could see a few colonial-era buildings. In the few months since publication, the book had gone out of date. A construction crew was finishing the display windows of a new car dealership.

I remembered what Mei had said about Shantou, about her father never coming back here.

The day was sunny but colder than I expected.

I stopped at a bakery and bought a pastry, a sort of danish. It didn't have the sweetness of a European danish—more breadlike, not the same mix of butter and glaze. I could get used to new ideas about pastries.

As I swallowed the last bite the sidewalk eroded into rubble. A man pushed a bicycle toward me, his face upturned with a quizzical look. When he opened his mouth I knew I would have no idea what he'd be talking about.

SUCCESS

E vie stirs the spaghetti sauce. I clear my throat and say, "Okay, listen to this. First chapter: Finding the Power Within":

> The vegetable cannery wasn't what the backers had described. I stood by the road looking at my new charge, on the verge of despair. Over the phone, they had portrayed a bustling new cannery, welcoming locals, access to Savannah's port and an excellent highway network. What I saw beside the two-rut track was a bootstrap operation.
> I had left a thriving shoe repair business—

"Thriving shoe repair business my ass," Evie says. "How can he say that?"

"Wait a second," I say. I continue: "—thriving shoe repair business with five stores in the St. Louis area to take on this start-up venture, and now I was filled with self-recrimination."

Evie tosses the wooden spoon into the sink with disgust, sending red spots blooming on the formica. In August our kitchenette is a walk-in oven, the heat intensified by my irritation that a family of three lives in a one-room apartment.

"How does he have the gall, is what I want to know."

"It *reads* okay, don't you think?" I rest the folder on my thigh.

She steps out onto the fire escape and lights a cigarette.

"I'm way too close," she says with a well-funneled vent of smoke. "Meaning, I'm in a position to remember that Roscoe was catatonic at the time. It was a *complete* fiasco, of his own making, and I had to pull him out of it."

"But if he came out of it with something that others can learn from—"

"That he can sell to schmucks," she says. "You know that's what Roscoe's counting on. God, I'm burning up in here."

She clenches her eyes tight. "I just *know* how he's going to paint me badly in this. 'My first wife, the needy—'" Evie breaks off. "Oh I don't know *what* he'll say. I just hope he doesn't include me at all."

"Maybe you're right," I say. "Maybe us reading this together is a bad idea."

My brother Roscoe met Evie in high school and they got together real young. Too young. They lived together for a couple of years outside St. Louis, and then they blew apart. I kept in touch with her, to make sure she was all right after they broke up, and one thing led to another. She came to San Antonio, eventually we got married. Roscoe was off jetting around the country. When he asked me to edit his book, I thought sure. It might mend a few fences, and we could use the money. But I should've thought more about Evie.

She shrugs.

"He just wants my professional opinion," I say.

I watch Evie pull plates down from the cupboard. "Right," she says. "And he's your brother."

"Doesn't mean we can't deal with each other like grown-ups," I say.

"Want to wash Cindy's hands? We're about ready."

Cindy is on our bed with her shells arranged for a tea party.

"Let's get ready for dinner," I say.

She thumps down on the carpet and in the bathroom reaches on her tiptoes to get her hands under the faucet. When we finish with her hands she soaps up mine, slathering the ink stains at the ends of my nails, rubbing her hands over the calluses on my left hand's fingertips.

"Does it hurt?" she says, poking the hard skin.

"No," I smile, "I don't feel a thing."

ROSCOE'S manuscript came in the mail covered with blue priority labels ten days ago, but I've just gotten into it. Although some parts grate on me as they did with Evie, other sections are surprisingly good, and I find myself applying his advice to my situation. The mental exercises for motivation, doing what you believe in rather than what gets (short-lived) approval from others, like my copy editor's salary. Change back from my twenty at the IGA, the coins in my palm. I *like* that feeling. But what Roscoe's book is saying is, I could do better.

Evie works afternoons at the co-op, so I pick up Cindy when I get off my shift at the newspaper and take her home, where I start going through Roscoe's manuscript. Many parts of it really need a full overhaul.

"But you've never done anything like that," Evie said the first night she saw me scratching the pages up. "We don't even *read* self-help books."

"It's okay, I've got it," I said. He agreed to pay my daily rate and I can work on it at home while I watch Cindy. We saw the place in Alamo Heights last week and the timing is perfect for getting a few grand.

When I reach the day-care that afternoon, Ruth the manager tells me Cindy has the sniffles and maybe I should take her to the doctor.

"She seems okay," I say. "You really think we need to see a doctor?" There's a shiny seam down the crease below Cindy's nose, but she's giggling and chasing two other little girls around the room.

"It's been going through here like wildfire," Ruth says. "Starts like this, then turns into a fever and tummy upsets."

"What can the doctor do?"

"Cindy should get a flu shot. Maybe you and your wife should too."

At home I give Cindy a handful of orange chewable vitamins and her pirate coloring book. I pull out Roscoe's manuscript. So far so good, and no mention of his first wife.

Breaking Free of Your Conscious Mind

You can turn off the No-sayer in you, and turn on the Yes. You can achieve the highest goals you set for yourself, but you may have to leave part of you behind. And that is the whipped dog part of your conscious self, the part that says, 'You haven't managed this before, what makes you think you can now?'

"Cindy, please stop bouncing on the bed, honey," I say. "Daddy's trying to work."

She laughs and throws her head back. She likes to see her brown hair fly around, it looks elegant. She keeps bouncing.

My main problem with Roscoe's book is I'm not sure how much to trust its facts. In editing, I'm not sure—should I just look for internal inconsistencies? Or should I go further and question parts that stop me cold? Points where I say, 'This didn't happen like this'? I should have cleared this up with Roscoe early on, but I didn't think of it. Now he's off helping a jewelry maker with re-organization in some remote corner of New Mexico, incommunicado. He'll come through the last week of August. By which time we'll really need to give Mr. Suarez a deposit on the place in Alamo Heights. If I can finish before Roscoe arrives, he can pay me for the editing, and boom, we'll plop his check down along with my check from the paper. And he'll be off to his publisher, he says.

So I go ahead and rework the parts that I'm not sure about.

When Mr. Suarez showed us the place, he got along well with Cindy, who was getting over a cold. Ordinarily I wouldn't let her out of the house like that but I was so worried that house was going to be snapped up, I just had to see it. But our upstairs neighbor bagged out on watching Cindy and I had to bring her along. She was cranky. Twice she did a spread-eagle on the floor (once on the kitchen linoleum and once on the wall-to-wall in the master bedroom), but Suarez just kept telling me about the new water heater, the A.C.'s efficiency because of the northern exposure, and something else that Cindy's bawling obliterated. Some people can't stay in the same room when she gets like that, but he has kids of his own. Three, he said. I convinced him to hold it for us, at least not sell before letting us counter-offer.

The place has two bedrooms—luxury compared to our efficiency—and a real kitchen, not a narrow path to a fire escape. Great windows, and a bath where Evie can stretch out after a day at the co-op. And Alamo Heights is a reasonable distance from her acupuncture clinic and a bus transfer from the paper's office. It'll be worth the stretch on our money, which is what Suarez says, of course, and which I tell Evie. I won't be editing copy forever. Before long I'll be doing columns, and someday having my screenplays produced.

"Mommy's home, Mommy's home!" Cindy leaps from the bed and lands with a surprisingly heavy thud. Her slight fever hasn't slowed her down. Out the window I see Evie coming up the walk, waving to a neighbor. It must be later than I think — six o'clock or so. I've gotten only three pages done this afternoon.

Going for Gold

> To achieve your goal, you have to keep a steady, clear focus on it. Visualize yourself enjoying the satisfaction of it. Here's how. As a boy, there was nothing I wanted more than to see the Chicago Cubs play at Wrigley Field. But a ticket cost too much, not to mention the El ticket. There was no way. My mother told me that. But I knew that if I focused all my energy on that one goal, if I could picture myself handing over the ticket to the ticket-taker at the park entrance, then I was halfway there...

"I was just looking over Chapter 3," I say, cradling the phone against my shoulder. "I love the opening story. I remember that. I think we might need to trim it a bit, though, so people follow the—"

"You know what I'm going for there, don't you?" Roscoe says.

"Sure, and most of the stories do their work of setting up an intimate space, but—"

"More than that," he says. I can hear the echoes of a hotel

lobby in the background. "I'm going for concrete examples that people can say, 'Hey, I know this guy.'"

I stir the sauce with the wooden spoon and nod. "Right, but you need to keep the reader moving toward the— Yeah. We can talk about it when you get here. Which is when, by the way?" I look over at Evie, frowning at me.

"Thursday? Sure, we'll pick you up," I say, with a big shrug. Evie shakes her head vigorously. "Which flight?"

"Hold on a sec," he says.

I grab a piece of paper from the junk drawer and write down the number. "Got it. You want to talk to Evie?"

"How is she?"

"Hi Roscoe," she says firmly, walking with the phone into the bedroom.

I meant to broach the topic of payment, but in the confines of the kitchen, with the heat and all, I can't. Plus, money is one of the things my brother and I hardly ever talk about. I decide to wait until I pick him up at the airport, which is right next to Alamo Heights. We can swing past the new place on the way home, an entrepreneurial move to show him what he's getting part of with his payment.

"I thought he wasn't coming until next week," I say to Evie when she comes back into the kitchen.

"Things in New Mexico went faster than he thought." She places the phone back on its base. "I couldn't tell if that's good or bad. And he claims to have to meet with *his publisher.*" She makes finger quotes in the air.

"Thursday. Damn, that puts me in a pinch," I say. "I've still got ten chapters to go."

She blows on the sauce and takes a slurp. "Don't worry

about having it done when he gets here. Mmm, this is good. When he comes we'll have to put Cindy in with us and move that plant out because of his allergy."

"Right, but I want it *nearly* done," I say. "Can you watch her tonight? I can get more done at the library."

"Mike, I'm whipped. Work here tonight, we won't bother you."

"Please, Evie?" I ladle the sauce out over the pasta.

"Really," she says, "he doesn't need to see it done. *He* never finishes anything on time."

"It would make me feel better," I say. "Please."

"You know," she says, taking in breath, "I really don't think this book thing is more important than our sanity. He can wait."

I try to think how to say that the house down payment is at least as important as one cozy night at home. Every way I try sounds angry.

"We'll need that down payment," I say, "and I don't want it as an advance. You know what he'd wring from that."

"Fine," she says. "I'll watch Cindy. Go to the library, or wherever."

I don't track down the whisp of innuendo in that 'wherever.' I grab my windbreaker. It's drizzling. By the time I reach the library, I'm so worked up over the new place and its possibilities that I can't concentrate. The manila folder with Roscoe's manuscript just seems way too much, especially with all those people milling around, browsing the magazine racks, asking the reference desk woman for help. Way too much information and possibility floating around for me to hunker down. I get through a few pages, then start a conversation with Roscoe in the car from the airport, about my plans for two screenplays—one based on our grandfather in San Diego, and one about lovers who underestimate each other.

THAT NIGHT I set the alarm for 3 a.m. and turn out the light. I think Evie is asleep but she says, "It's too much, what they're asking. If Suarez won't come down, we should walk."

Not what I want to hear. "And look how long for another house?"

We both are looking at the ceiling, its endless permutations.

"Till we find one."

I sigh.

"It's not like that location is ideal anyway."

"This is about something else," I say.

"What?"

"About me making more money. That I need to."

She palms her pillow flat so she can see me. "No it's not."

"I think it is."

"It's just that things come up. We're even afraid to take Cindy to the doctor." Her voice cracks.

"Not *afraid*. If she needs to go, I'll take her."

She doesn't say anything.

"In two months," I say, "they'll be taking on two new assistant editors and I'm up for one. Then we'll be glad we stretched ourselves."

"You sound like Roscoe."

"This is real," I say, careful to keep steady.

Trapezoids of light arc across the ceiling from the window. The sluish of a passing car dopplers on wet pavement.

"You sound just like Roscoe," she says. "Have it all. Just dream big enough."

I roll on my side and kiss her. Another car passes.

Your Place in the Sun

When you can see your goal achieved, vividly, you are nine-tenths of the way to achieving it. The reason many imaginative people fail to achieve the goal they envision is because they don't see what happens next. When I was in business school, the thing I wanted most in the world was a Corvette Stingray. I could see the car, canary yellow, in my driveway. I could even see my girlfriend's hair luffing in the passenger window. Yet I did not see myself writing the check to the car dealer, or any day-to-day connection that enabled me to act, no link to the world I lived in.

I'm running a half hour late getting out the door to meet Roscoe's plane. Ruth would not let me go without my promising to "take this little girl to a doctor." I feel her little forehead, she's fine, just a little warm. She does her starfish stretch to keep me from fastening the seatbelt.

"Cindy, please, Daddy has to pick up Uncle Roscoe at the airport. You don't want us to be late, do you?"

Sobs. "I don't care!"

"You don't mean that. You haven't seen him for a long time. He can't wait to see you."

Roscoe doesn't know how to react to Cindy. During his visits he talks to her in a strange voice, one that Evie says made her skin crawl from childhood guilt trauma. Hoping it was just a matter of their getting used to each other, I tried leaving Roscoe and Cindy together during his last visit, while I ran a piece into the editor. When I got back, Roscoe was pacing the edge of the parking lot in front of our apartment. He rushed me.

"Thank God you're back," he said. "I'd rather be left with a caged lion."

If I could get Cindy to the babysitter next door, that would make Roscoe more at ease during the drive through Alamo Heights. But that means a ten-minute detour on top of being a half hour late. What are the odds Roscoe will still be at the terminal?

We finally get started and I hit the gas. We race along 410 East and as we approach the airport exit I realize I haven't dropped off Cindy after all. Change of plans.

Roscoe strides out of the automatic sliding glass door in his usual train of swinging briefcase, rolling carry-on and cell phone. His tie is loose and his wiry hair is in its evening dandelion mode. Through an illusion, the assortment of people entering and leaving the airport appear to be shooting off him like sparks or debris. He's looking around, his chin raised.

Leaning against the car, I flag him down.

"Mike, I was set to take a cab," he says. He must realize his voice sounded hard, because then he chuckles.

"Sorry we're late, Cindy's fighting a cold," I say. "Great to see you."

We have an awkward hug and get his things into the trunk. He kneels into the backseat to give Cindy a kiss. "Remember Uncle Roscoe, Cindy?" he says.

"No!" she shouts. Standing behind Roscoe, I can see her little white boots kick out with the force of it.

"Sure you do." I turn to Roscoe. "She's hot and cranky. Let's get out of the traffic pattern here. Say," I pause as if an idea has just come over me. "We're not far from the place we're thinking of moving to. Wanna swing by there and you can have a look?"

"Sounds great. Maybe another time," Roscoe says. "I'm beat, and I need to make a few follow-up calls someplace quiet. I was dodging bullets the whole time in Albuquerque."

"This place is on the way. Besides," I say, "I'd really like your take on it before we make a bid."

He shrugs. I can see the bags under his eyes. "If you want. I have no idea about real estate here, but—"

"You've got a sense. It'd make me feel better," I say.

"Let's go then."

Cindy quiets down after we get back on 410, but that's just for two exits. I'm thinking through whether we can find Suarez and get him to let us see the inside again.

"So how's Evie?" he says on the exit ramp. He wipes his eyes with the splayed thumb and forefinger of his right hand.

"She's great, she can't wait to see you."

"I'll bet." He smiles sidelong. His eyes sweep from me out the windshield to the woman sitting impatiently at the bus stop. "She hasn't been anxious to see me since we were in high school."

"And she still loves you."

"In her way."

I'm thinking about five blocks. Should I buzz Suarez from the front or call him from the office? Out of Roscoe's earshot would be best, so I can explain his backing role to Suarez in vague terms.

"Albuquerque," I say, when I notice it has gotten quiet. "I've never been there." Cindy is being surprisingly quiet in the back. She bounces against her carseat as if she has a song in her head.

"It's all right. I'd rather talk about your work. About *our* work." He laughs. "How's our book coming?"

"Oh, it's been a joy," I lie, make a left turn. One thing I've learned in editing is to punch the good news first, and hard. "I really enjoy it. You've struck just the right tone —"

"Watch out." A Firebird zags out of the right lane in front of us.

"We can discuss it later," I say.

He seems nonplussed, suddenly distracted. "What neighborhood is this?"

"It's called Alamo Heights."

"I should've known."

"Here it is." I slow along the curb.

The late afternoon light hits the wall a warm yellow, the lintel above the front door casting a sidelong shadow. It looks hopeful. I remember it more impressive from the back.

"Daddy I'm hu-u-ngry," chirps Cindy.

"We'll get you something to eat in a little bit," I say. "Right now we're going to see our new house. Isn't that exciting?"

"I'm *hu-u-u-u-ngry*."

"Wait here with Uncle Roscoe and I'll see if Mr. Suarez is in." Before Roscoe can protest I am up the sidewalk and into the brick management building.

Inside the lobby I look over to Suarez's office and the door is closed, as usual. I ask the woman at the reception desk if I can use her phone to call him.

She says only if I can tell the operator how to connect to Hell.

"Just kidding," she says. "Tomorrow would be better."

I walk slowly back to the car. Roscoe is leaning against it. He has all four windows closed, and his left hand sandwiched under his right armpit.

"She bit me," he says.

Learning to Accept Fate

When your dreams become reality, they may not always resemble your initial vision. Then it's time to adapt to their real-life expression, and find the blend of vision and reality that works. After a year, the South Carolina cannery was a success, but not the way I first imagined. Did that mean it was a failure? No. Did it mean my initial vision didn't account for all possible variables? Most definitely.

"Evie, we're home," I call into the apartment. "Evie?"

She comes out of the bedroom with her head tilted back, a washcloth on her forehead.

"Are you all right?" I say.

"Hiya darling," Roscoe says, arms wide, moving past me.

"Hi Ros. I've got a killer headache."

"I'm sorry."

"How was your flight?"

"It was okay." Roscoe hugs her, his eyes roaming the apartment. "I need to make some calls."

"You can use our room," I say. I turn to Evie. "We went by the house. Suarez wasn't there, so we just walked around the outside."

"Like burglars," Roscoe says from the kitchenette.

"Don't look around in there!" Evie calls, her eyes on the wall above my head.

"My eyes are sealed," Roscoe yells back.

"You can see the golf course from the backyard," I say to Evie. "I was standing under that big oak in back, looking over and I could see a slice of the course. It's fantastic. It had a really good feeling. My dad would love it."

"I'm hot," Cindy says.

"Maybe *he* can buy it. It's over-priced." She turns to Cindy. "You feel hot? Lemme see." She puts a hand to her forehead. "She doesn't *feel* hot. I can't believe you prowled around the place."

"We didn't prowl. It was daylight. We didn't break in or anything. I just wanted Roscoe to see the place."

"He talked about scaling the fence," Roscoe says as he enters the living room.

"You're kidding," Evie says. Her eyes do that dramatic upward swing.

"I followed him around the side because he insisted, with the late afternoon sun. I was just admiring the nice tree in the yard. But Mike," Roscoe laughs, "he said, 'Let's just climb over, you can't see the bay window from here.' He had his hands set like a stirrup to give me a boost."

"Mike—"

"We didn't do it," I shrug. "Suarez wasn't around. I wanted Roscoe to see." I turn to Roscoe. "So you got through?"

"Yeah."

"Everything okay?"

"Great. They still have to present it to the board. A formality." He takes a big breath and claps his hands together. "So! Can I take you two to dinner? Or, Mike—did you want to talk about the book first?"

"We can't do dinner out. Cindy's getting over a fever." Evie blows her bangs. "I was going to make something here."

"Perfect."

"So Roscoe," she says, taking a breath, "how have you been?"

"Good, Evie. I've been doing real good. I met a nice girl, we've been seeing each other."

"Yeah?" Evie's eyebrows go up. "What's she like?"

"Oh," Roscoe laughs. "You know my type by now."

"Tell me anyway."

"She's five eight, slim, dark hair to here." He angles his hand to his neck. "Very attractive."

"That does sound familiar. And you two are happy?"

"So far." He gives a goofball grin, shrugs.

Evie smiles back. "Why don't you two talk about the book and I'll put something together," she says.

"Works for me," Roscoe says. "So," he said as the two of us sat on the couch, "how much time have you put in on it?"

I pause. "Fifteen days, give or take."

"Fifteen, let's see, that comes to—"

I mouth the number.

"Three thousand dollars," Roscoe says, looking up. "That what we talked about?"

"It is."

"Now I have a question for you."

I tense.

"Would you be willing to invest that into something that would give you a fivefold return?" he says.

I hear wind through the grass. "Well in fact, that's exactly what I—what we plan to do," I say. "We'd put that money toward a down payment on the condo we saw this afternoon."

Roscoe looks nonplussed. "I'm talking about a real investment," he says. "You don't live in an investment. And, correct me if I'm wrong, but you don't see triple-digit returns in real estate. I'm talking about a share of royalties."

"What I really want," I say, "is a better place to live and work. And the place we saw—" I smile.

"See, the book needs stonger narrative," Roscoe says. "I'll give you a free hand. Make the storytelling more dramatic. Move some scenes around, maybe. You're the writer in the family. And for that you'd get royalty share." He smiles. "I know in self-publishing the word 'royalty' doesn't sound impressive, but the deal I've struck with these distributors should be a nice chunk of change."

"Self-publishing? The investment I need now is like, more space," I laugh. "Where I can work better. Here, the heat, the construction. I can't get enough done."

Roscoe nods, then squints. He waves his hand over the marked up manuscript, which he hasn't had time to peruse. "Think of the arc of your life, not just the next five years."

"You two big thinkers ready?" Evie calls.

"You should've seen him, Evie," Roscoe says as we move to the table. He points at me. "He really wanted to climb over the fence."

"Ros, you're such a spoilsport." Evie passes the pasta.

"What's a spoil-sport?" Cindy asks.

"It's someone who's no fun," I say.

"Someone who's no fun?"

"Someone who shells out three grand for grammatical corrections but won't jump over a fence," Roscoe says. He laughs bitterly. "Just kidding, Mike. Worth every penny."

"No fun," Evie says. "Like you were."

"What's grammatical mean?"

"How *was* I then?" Roscoe says.

"No fun. Not there. You weren't there. You've changed," Evie adds quickly. "You're better now. You ask about other people. But Jesus, *then*. That time you forgot I was at the train station—"

"Christ, forever that."

"So—different subject," I say, waving a hand across a mime's chalkboard, "does your Albuquerque business have anything to do with publishing?"

"No," Roscoe says. "Strictly consulting. For—"

"No business talk at the dinner table," Evie says.

"What's *grammatical* mean?" Cindy rocks in her chair.

"The weather's lovely," Roscoe says. He flashes a fake grin, eyes nearly closed.

I laugh.

"Is that a restriction?" Evie says. "Is that all there is? Business and the weather." Then she shoots her eyes my way. "Mike, don't pretend that's *you*. I know *you* don't agree with that."

Roscoe turns to me, eyebrows raised.

Cindy looks at me too. "What's grammatical?"

"He was joking," I say. "Roscoe knows there's more to life than work."

"Sure," he concedes. He dabs his mouth with his napkin. "A lot more. But you know, nothing takes as much work as work. And that's because Evie, for a man, work is the path to excellence, to fulfillment."

"That's what we're talking about," Evie say. "That's why you're alone here saying that. That's why you can't— Tell Mike about that part of *fulfillment*. About driving people away."

I feel like the two of them are suddenly alone in the room. Roscoe looks almost hurt. "I'm seeing a woman now."

"What I mean," I say to Roscoe, "is there's a balance—"

"Sure, sure, balance," he cuts in with a wave of his hand. "The middle way. It's just a book. Like Tom Clancy or *War and Peace*. There's lots of books. Evie, don't get your panties in a knot."

"You bastard. You haven't changed at all." Evie runs into the kitchen.

"Mommy?"

"What'd I say?" Roscoe's palms turn up.

"Roscoe, just—" I say. "Stop."

"What did I say?"

Our eyes lock, and then he flinches away. The swinging door, the whole scene, is slowing down.

"Evie?" I follow her. She's leaning against the counter, lighting a cigarette.

"I'll be all right," she says, wiping her face. "You go back in and make nice with him. I just need a minute." She takes a breath. "You're so different from him, so much—" She looks up, and in her glance I understand that the difference is what she loves about me and also what puts me down a notch in her gauge of life's chances.

"I love you," I say.

"I know," she laugh-sobs. "Go tell him what that's like."

Angelina Before the Throne of Heaven

W HEN Roger appeared this morning after the nine o'clock chimes, he looked like he had seen the spirits at last. His rufous hair was shocked straight up and wispy, like he'd been raking his hands through it.

"She's been here two days, but I haven't told anybody," he said to Marcus in front of the bus where Marcus lived. "To tell the truth, I was surprised she really came. Her name's Angelina. But she won't say a word."

A full-grown woman with eyes and legs and hands, and a red blouse. She had walked up to the sign Roger was holding at the arrival gate of the Charlotte airport, a sign that said in bleeding blue magic marker, 'Angelina.' As if by writing the sign he had called her up, a genie.

"Just like a genie," Roger repeated. "I full expected to drive home from the airport by myself. I knew I was a big old fool as soon as I sent in the check to that agency. But I chalked it off as two thousand lotto tickets. Which is how I convinced myself to mail it off in the first place."

He explained all this to Marcus, following him around back to the shed.

Marcus erupted with a startled guffaw, mopped his face on his sleeve, threw open the shed, and looked up at his opus, the Throne of Heaven. It bridled in the steamy dim interior, its proportions locked in conflict (the massive cathedra vs. the tiny figures), clanking up against Cray's disker and the rusted pruning saw hanging from a nail in the green fiberglass wall.

The height of the Throne's persimmon seat suits the Spirits' posterior. From the long, narrow beam of the backrest, the wings rise up in sheaths of crinolated blue aluminum foil. The tableau of bottle-cap characters and wooden animals turns the shed into a vessel ready to bear Them away from the world's midday weariness. And for that They owe their servant Marcus, a fifty-one-year-old Caucasian male with few distinguishing markings.

You could see his mind working on the puzzle Roger described: it pulled his eyebrows together and made his nose long. With his Willie Nelson hair, you can see why the Spirits chose Marcus to create their designs in the shed. (Or you may disbelieve in their very existence, like his sister Evelyn, who laughs at his carvings and bottle-cap sculptures. You might not even acknowledge the perversity of matter when, say, you're trying to hang a picture, struggling up on your tiptoes, and the wire refuses to loop over the nail just beyond your grasp. Fine. Go ahead.) When he gets that steely look in his eye, like a coveted marble, it's a forbidding sight.

He was thinking, *Lord have mercy, he did it. Roger bought somebody.* Then Marcus accepted it because things happen and go right on happening. There's no seam. You never hear of the world stopping because it got too strange.

"You've been talking it for some time, haven't you?" Marcus

said. "Just a month ago you said it again. 'Marcus, it's time I got a family.'" He shook his head.

It took a while, but Roger finally got Marcus to climb in and they drove back to Roger's place: a low brick-and-siding rambler east of town, shoved back from the road just before it peters out. The houses on either side are ramblers, varying mainly in their patterns of brick and siding. They have the same front yards, empty except for the tractor tire filled with plants. Alongside Roger's house stood a green fiberglass shed shaped like a little barn.

A lawn jockey in a faded red plaster jacket shook his fist by the driveway as Roger pulled the truck up the gravel.

The engine shuddered dead.

"I sure hope you can help," Roger said in the new silence. "I think I love her."

Roger's house had a bachelor's hard corners. Inside the front door it was dark as a cave, with posters of long, sleek Jaguars framed in silver-colored metal. A fake leather couch—brownish-black—and a green shag rug stretched from the front room back to the kitchen doorway. Piles of *Penthouse*, *Muscle*, and other magazines with big-wheel trucks teetered off the pine coffee table. A beige shirt was wedged between two cushions on the couch.

"It's just," Roger was telling Marcus for the fourteenth time, "that she hasn't said a word since the airport. I don't know if she's homesick, or what all."

His lip curled up with a new idea. "She may be deaf!"

Marcus made another sweep with his eyes, then said, "Where is she?"

"Where is she? Marcus, she's gone!" But just as Roger cried

out, they heard noises from the back. Low voices, music.

"She likes t.v.," said Roger, laughing sheepishly. "Two days that's all she wants is t.v. Hey, Angelina."

Planted in a plastic chair, facing the portable television on the counter, was a compact body in jeans and red flowered shirt, black-blue hair flowing like a fountain from the top. She didn't turn around when they came into the room and Roger said again, ridiculously upbeat, "Hey Angelina."

He walked over and switched off the t.v. just as a fabric softener burst on the screen with swelling volume.

"I want you to meet a friend of mine. This is Marcus, he lives closer to town." Roger's eyes darted over to Marcus for confirmation.

But Marcus didn't see him. He couldn't get past the woman's wide face, the color of maple. Her nose was almost flat, and her lips were full but only in the middle, like they had been pinched open from the sides. The only part of her face that moved was the live dark eyes—they made his stomach light. They had so much white, and no border between the pupil and the iris, so the whole circles hit him with the force of buckshot—they were Terésa's eyes. No doubt about it.

Those eyes told Marcus that Terésa had found Huntersville from that other world, the Not Here, the New York. From twelve years ago. But she had needed a different body to get here.

Marcus was still breathing, and otherwise things were the same as before. Roger was still talking.

"Marcus knows lots of things," Roger said with conviction. "You want to know about some place in America, he's probably been there. Memphis, Montana, Chicago, New Orleans. He makes stuff, too," said Roger. "Crazy stuff, and paintings. You'll like his paintings, they got colors wild as your shirt. And he's handy."

With the t.v. screen blank, Angelina's eyes followed Roger, glancing to Marcus only for a few seconds each time Roger nodded his way.

In a lower voice, Roger said, "See, I know she understands English, the ad guaranteed it. But she hasn't said a word since the airport. She couldn't have gotten to Charlotte if she didn't speak English, right? San Francisco's a big airport, isn't it? That's where she changed planes. She woulda had to talk to *somebody*."

"Habla English?" said Marcus.

Silence.

"Shit, I've already asked her that. She ain't Spanish anyhow."

"They speak it lots of other places too," Marcus growled.

"In Asia? She come from the Philippines." Roger sighed. "Hell, I guess it was crazy to drag you over here, Marcus." He looked again at the silent woman. "I'm sorry. I just thought—"

The woman held up a hand with her fingers close together. "Yes."

Roger froze, glaring at her. "That's the first thing—"

"You speak English? So this man is your husband now?" Marcus was saying, leaning forward. The word made a faint gurgle in his throat. "Marido. Comprendo?"

"No!" It was a rush of air. She unbolted something from her eyes, then like a stone had been rolled away from her mouth, words launched out, several different languages, with rolling r's and snakelike s's. It was like three people talking fast instead of one. While this kept up, she grabbed a big black shoulder bag and poked her hand around in it. The hand came out with a slip of yellow paper which she kept flicking with her forefinger. Neither Marcus nor Roger could see what the paper said, it flashed around too fast. First in the kitchen, then the front room. They followed her. After a long minute Marcus said, "I think she's saying *made*."

"What?" Roger squinted.

"I— she's saying she came to be your maid."

"Yes!" cried Angelina.

"Maid?" Roger's forehead wrinkled. "I don't have a maid."

"Maid!" said Angelina. "Not married."

"I can't afford a maid. I don't need a maid. I need companionship. What's she pointing at?"

"Okay, okay now," said Marcus, walking toward her slowly with his palms out. "Donde yo el papiera, por favor," he said. He stole a glance at her ankles.

"This is the damnedest . . ." grumbled Roger behind him. "I'm gonna write that company, boy. They can bite my ass."

"No wife! No!" Angelina yelled, then a few more rolling r's, then, very clearly, "Maid!"

"Shit, I don't need a maid. Does it look like I need a maid?" He waved an arm around the living room, let it fall against his jeans with a slap.

Marcus studied the piece of paper—typed. "It says here 'employee,'" he said. "You know what that means don't you, Roj?"

The woman nodded firmly. "Maid!" she said.

"Looks like you two are communicating," Marcus said. His

chest and neck muscles were numb and hard from the effort of keeping his arm from shooting out and punching Roger. How dare he yell at Terésa—after she had taken twelve years to find her way here! Not to mention *buying* her! Marcus had never dreamt it this way. He needed to get home, lie down, sort things out.

"Where are you going?" Roger whined. "Wait, Marcus, you gotta help me!"

"I need to get home."

"Marcus!"

"How is it you can afford a wife but not a maid?"

Roger's face went blank, he stared at the fake leather couch. "It's that—" he started. "Well I'd have to pay a maid every month. The agency said I could pay in installments, every other month." He shoved his hands deep in his pockets and looked outside. "Besides, I had my heart *set*," he whined.

"Maid!"

Marcus shrugged. "I'm sure I don't know."

His mind was flying off to the caps he found yesterday by the dumpster behind the post office: the old Coke caps with baseball players under the clear rubber seal, a kind they hadn't made for 15 years or so. Back when he was Up North. He scratched his stomach, recalling Terésa's coral cafeteria uniform, the white apron. Then the thought that she had been bought by Roger returned, and shot a hot acid plume up his windpipe.

"I gotta be going. You two have a lot to get straight."

Roger shook his head. "This is the damnedest mess. You want something to eat? I got some doughnuts."

Marcus considered the doughnuts as he set out the door.

The gravel was blinding gray, it would be a long walk but it would steady his heart from fluttering. The jockey gave him the fist. Marcus returned it. For the struggle.

The straw grass of the ditch spoked against his trousers.

"Well hold on," came Roger's voice from the pickup, slowing alongside. "I'll drive you back, if you're gonna abandon me."

Marcus looked up at the truck. The woman was on the seat beside Roger. Marcus squinted back up the road. "I'll walk."

"No you won't."

Angelina's eyes were darting all around—the dashboard, the road, Marcus' trousers as he climbed up beside her. Her jeans stretched over her thighs taut as flesh. Marcus suddenly felt withered by the feelings he was having. The squared-off brick primary school passed by, the basketball courts empty except for one boy dribbling.

"So," said Marcus when the silence had become ridiculous, "you come from the Pacific?"

"Baguio. Baguio City," she said.

"Baguio. Isn't that in South America?" said Roger. "Wait, though, the Pacific . . ." His hands were doing figures against the steering wheel. "Hell," he said with a laugh, "my geography's terrible. It was always so early in the morning and I sat in the back of the class. Marcus, you remember I used to do chores for Doctor Lawsom?" he said, leaning forward to talk past Angelina. "He'd need wood split by six every morning. I'd be out back of his place, and see the stars and planets as it got light. Could see them through my breath sometimes. You know about that, Angie? Ever see your breath in Baguio?"

Roger had worked himself loose, Marcus could tell.

The woman didn't say anything. Marcus shifted on the seat, her thigh touched his. The windshield was frying him. Something very wrong was happening. Why did he leave her back in New York? It was all muddy now.

They passed the prison, and he smelled the long grass and rubbed his hands together.

"Speak of the devil," said Roger, and honked the horn. "Hey, Dr. Lawsom!"

An ancient with a cane was walking beside the road with a young woman in white. With wide eyes he watched the pickup descend on him, offering his open hand as it passed.

* * *

"I LOVED HER," he says up at the Throne, looking shocked. He says it again, slowly: "Marcus loved his best friend's woman in another world. How could I *do* that?"

Terésa had liked him all right, too, twelve years ago, back in New York. She had been so sweet to him it made his palms sweat. Marcus took her out to the island where the big lady in the nightgown looked for burglars. That's what he told her, and she laughed. Together looking out at the rough grey surface of the water, and the seagulls creeling up in the air, screaming.

"She is so big and powerful," said Terésa, "so beautiful."

They held hands on the ferry, he kept prying loose to wipe his palms on his trousers and look around at other people, very serious, and she laughed at him. Her black hair blew around her face, she caught a strand and pulled it back. She had a wide comet tail of teeth when she laughed. Marcus couldn't think for looking at the nylons on Terésa's ankles, her squared off black shoes.

* * *

They reached the drive. Roger pulled off onto the grass behind the chocked school bus and cut the engine.

Marcus swallowed, looking out the pickup's windshield at his home, the signs he had painted himself, the wood-and-steel bear perched on the embankment. He looked peaked.

"Well," he said, clearing his throat, "can I get you two something? A mason jar, Roger?"

"No thanks. We should get back and talk this out—"

But the woman had slid down from the truck after Marcus.

"Well," said Roger, throwing his door open, "maybe so." Angelina looked at him. "Beer," he said. "Do you want beer?"

She nodded.

"I also got water," said Marcus.

"She wants a mason jar like me." As they followed him up the steps onto the bus, Terésa paused to touch the neck of the bottle-cap doe.

Marcus went to the back and scuffled there with the jars and bottles on the floor. When he came back with the drinks, she was holding the madonna, the one he had done remembering her. She was cradling it like a child, running her hand against the edge. The triad of mason jars trembled in his hands, glass edges singing. She looked at him with blank wisdom, her shoulders sloped with the strength he meant for the madonna.

Something inside him gave way like a rotten plank.

"You got a handful," said Roger, nodding at the glasses clinking between Marcus' fingers. "I got this one. Here you go, Angelina. Bottoms up."

"What do you reckon she makes of all this?" Marcus whispered.

"Damned if I know what to make of it myself," said Roger, sipping his beer. "I thought that's why you did it. To confuse folks."

Marcus' face went slack. "Sorry it's not cold. I don't have an ice box," he told the woman, seeing her lips flush wider in a rubbery sour face after her first sip. "I wanted to run a line out to the bus a couple of years back, but Duke Power said it wasn't grounded."

"Sometimes," said Roger, taking a seat on the pallet in the bus' midsection, "it seems that they made that big old lake for no earthly purpose except fishing. Which is a good reason, except for all those houses at the bottom of it."

"Where are my manners?" barked Marcus. He started brushing off a spot beside Roger on the pallet. "Here, Terésa, here's a seat."

"Her name's Angie. Angelina."

Instead of sitting where Marcus pointed, she walked to the front of the bus and lowered herself in the driver's seat, staring out the windshield at the road to Charlotte.

"Aw c'mon, honey, we don't have to talk the wife maid thing now. Let's just have a little beer, nice and relaxed."

"You sound real natural talking that way, Roger. Have you been practicing?" Marcus grinned. "'Aw, c'mon honey,'" he mimicked, extra saccharine, then dropped his voice. "Except she ain't your wife."

It was quiet except for the German shepherd barking across the street. There was no breeze through the bus, and sweat was beading on Roger's forehead.

"Why don't you show her the throne?" he said.

"The throne," Marcus blinked hard. "Hey, uh—Angie, you

want to see what I'm making?" Then he added in a low voice, "What I left New York to make?"

She started out of the driver's seat and followed him down the steps.

SHE NEARLY ran into Gabriel of the Last Days when she entered the shed.

"Come in, come in." Marcus made an eager sweep of his hand.

But she stopped at the doorway. She ducked her head and moved forward slowly, her hand before her face as if to catch cobwebs. Inside was dark.

As her eyes adjusted to the darkness after the fiery daylight (the wonder of this shed as an exhibit site is not just its unex-pectedness but its slow-dawning effect), the silvery glitter appeared to her like flames against the back wall. The light burned and formed foil-covered wings, and slowly the dark wood of the throne's backrest materialized between them. Then the foil flared and divided into two colors—silver and violet—and candles sprang from the armrests. Her lips parted.

The light from the doorway was now enough to reveal the smaller figures at the left of the upper daïs—robes and wings. She smiled, then turned and laughed at the one she had nearly run into—the one with big eyebrows raised, wearing gardener's greens under his angel gown, his face screwed up savagely against his trumpet's embouchure, eyes vanished in a grimace.

"You like that one?" said Marcus eagerly. "Yeah, he's, he's, he's a character, Gabriel."

She nodded, her eyes already moving down to the angry-looking man with the broad-brimmed hat. In one claw-like hand he gripped a thick book, the other jabbed threateningly at the roof. At his feet a bald man was on his knees, hands clasped together, maw gaping up, begging.

Behind the bald man, larger than the other figures, a voluptuous woman stood robed from the waste down, wearing only a black bra above. She stared down her nose, her wide eyes icy like a ghost, unsmiling, not angry, her left hand on the bald man's shoulder, her right holding a crescent-shaped sickle high above.

Angelina tilted her head to one side.

Behind the tall woman and to the right, against the shed wall where a large augur hung like a monstrous corkscrew, huddled another, larger figure, also wood—a hunched, menacing blob.

"That's the bruin of betrayal," Marcus explained. She started at the sound of his voice.

"Sorry," he said. "The bruin of betrayal roams the sky, searching for weak hearts. When he finds one, he claws it open like a hive of honey. He's not finished yet, when he's done he'll look like the one out front. See?" He pointed out the door to the bear near the ditch.

All along the front of the lower, foot-high platform stood assorted items—rows and rows of shotgun shells (she hadn't seen so many since Marcos rounded up all the guns in the countryside when she was a little girl), some shards of blue porcelain, a corkscrew with painted flames, and one whole plate, ringed with gold, bearing a pastel portrait of Elvis Presley.

"It's a trick I learned from a guy named Raphael," Marcus was saying, still looking at the bear. "He made a model of everything he planned to fit into his big murals before he made them. It's good practice, and helps prevent mistakes." His head bobbed with conviction.

Circling up further to the right, her gaze fell on four or five plywood figures, each painted in three colors, different combinations of green, blue, and red.

"They're not done yet either," said Marcus suddenly, following her eyes. "Those're just rough starts for the does. Don't even look at them yet, they'll change so much."

Next to them Angelina spotted a female with black hair, a red print dress, deep blue skin.

She was beginning to feel light-headed from the hurly-burly of all the figures and the airless shed. Suddenly she didn't know where to look. It was too much.

That's when they descended—ghostly flocks, flying through the air toward the back of the shed, suddenly filling the skies, painted in a blocky hand. Some were placed so that they held up the hand-drill, the augur, the rake and other tools that hung around the walls, bearing them away as offerings, their white robes and long hair flapping and fluttering behind. Like the angels, she thought, or the spirits that came to sleeping Filipino children and sat on their chests till they stopped breathing. She could hear her mother's voice explaining.

Their incessant wings kicked up the suffocating fumes of paint and paint thinner and gasoline, but the man with long hair was standing behind her blocking the doorway, she couldn't get out.

Beside the throne, to the right of the little stool, she spotted the baptismal font from her father's church in Baguio. It was wooden and eight-sided, like a large old lantern, and rested on a plant-like base that tapered from four sides to a rough round stem. It, too, was covered in silver and violet and red foil; bits of white paper with handwritten words dangled from its sides.

The crowd of statues and relics before her jostled for her attention, swirling and shoving like an airport mob. The angels taxiing beyond, bearing off to Manila, one by one. She wanted to give them a message to take, her uncle in Manila could get it to her parents, but she couldn't think. This place.

She was gulping in big mouthfuls of bad air. Tiny pins stabbed her vision in blurry arcs. She turned to the door once more—blind to the messages painted on the riser of the daïs— and felt all the live things behind her, calling her with their eyes, flailing soundlessly like the wind from beating wings.

Outside, back in America, the man was following her.

"I know it's not much to show for twelve years," Marcus said with an embarrassed laugh. "Still and all . . ." He turned back to close the fiberglass door.

"Wonderful," she said, choking on the spring air.

She didn't say anything else, but Marcus looked at her like she was about to. "Yeah?" he said.

She moved her head like she wanted to ask a question. Instead, her eyes raked his face as if trying to reconcile it with what she'd just seen inside the shed.

"You understand, don't you?" he said. "You see why I did it?"

She still didn't say anything, but embarrassed by his gaze, she laughed.

"She's speechless," Roger said. "Marcus, you've gone and undone all our morning's work, getting her to open up."

CPSIA information can be obtained
at www.ICGtesting.com
Printed in the USA
LVOW11s1554200717

542032LV00001B/203/P